99 fables by
william march

99 fables by william march

edited with an introduction by

william t. going

illustrated by richard brough

1960
university of alabama press

THE LIBRARY
OF ALABAMA
CLASSICS

The University of Alabama Press
Tuscaloosa, Alabama 35487-0380
All rights reserved
Manufactured in the United States of America

∞

Library of Congress Cataloging-in-Publication Data

March, William, 1893–1954.
  99 fables, by William March [pseud.] Edited with an introd. by William T. Going; illustrated by Richard Brough.
      p. cm.
  Originally published under title: I rode with the Ku Klux Klan.
  London : Arco Publishers, 1954. With new introd.
  ISBN 978-0-8173-5685-9 (pbk. : alk. paper) — ISBN 978-0-8173-8585-9
(electronic) [University, Ala.] University of Alabama Press, 1960.
    PS3505.A53157 N5

                                                            60008101

acknowledgments

WITHOUT TWO SUMMER
grants-in-aid from the Research Committee of the University of Alabama this edition would not have been possible. Nor would it have been possible without the full co-operation of the heirs, trustee and executor of the estate of the late William Edward March Campbell. I am especially indebted to the following persons who have encouraged me in this undertaking and who allowed me to use their typescripts of the Fables: Mrs. Patty Campbell Maxwell, Mrs. Margaret Campbell Jones, and Mr. Paul Strickland. Each of these copies is unique, and together they have formed the bases of the present text.

In addition, I have received valuable counsel and guidance from Mr. J. Finley McRae and Mr. M. B.

Slaughter of The Merchants National Bank of Mobile; Mr. and Mrs. Nicholas S. McGowin of Mobile; Miss Marion Davenport of Fairhope; Mrs. Marie Campbell Haley and Mrs. C. E. McCrory of Tuscaloosa; Mr. and Mrs. Peter Campbell of New York; and Mr. Ivan von Auw, Jr., of Harold Ober Associates, New York.

The following magazines and newspapers, which I gratefully acknowledge, printed earlier versions of these fables: *Accent* (The Young Poet and the Worm, The Stableboy, The Screech Owl and the Farmer), *Kansas Magazine* (Aesop and King Croesus, The Prayer That Was Almost Answered, The Fisherman and the Hen, The Nightingale That Listened to Men, The King and the Plotters, The Wolves and the Work Animals, The Monkey Hill, The Distinguished and the Obscure), *Prairie Schooner* (The Persimmon Tree, The Peacock and His Bride, The Woodcutter and the Lion, Men and the Other Animals, The Slave and the Cart Horse, The Proud Queen, The Shepherd and His Monument, The Tears of the Rich, The Hangman and the Hero, The Mink and the Tame Animals, The Strangers, The Unique Quality of Truth), *Rocky Mountain Review* (The Elephants and the Antelopes, The Traitorous Jackal, The Doubting Ducks, Cowards and Fearless Men, The Mongoose and the Cobra, The Criminal Female, The Visitor and the Razorback Hogs), *Tanager* (The Farmer Boy and the Ladies, The Magician and the Peasants, The King and the Bright Young Men, The

Miracle, The Panther and the Woodcutter, Man and His Natural Enemy, The Untouchable, Aesop's Last Fable, The Fat Woman and the Terrier, The Prophets and the Mountains), *University Review* (The Democratic Bretts), *The Old Line* (The Escaped Elephant), *New York Sun* (The Gull and the Earthquake), *New York Post* (The Pig and the Dirty Doves, The Wild Horses, The Crow and the Parrot).

W. T. G.

contents

introduction

died in 1954, the longest unpublished manuscript among
his papers was this collection of fables. It was first
assembled "about 1938," when William Edward March
Campbell had just retired as vice-president of the
Waterman Steamship Corporation, which in eighteen
years he had helped to build from a small Mobile line
to one of the world's largest. He was forty-five, and he
had seen much of life when as William March he settled
down in a Manhattan apartment "to write as I please."

Behind him were his boyhood days in Mobile, Pensa-
cola, and the small sawmill towns of Alabama and
Florida. His attendance at Valparaiso University and
the University of Alabama had been all too brief. When

the United States entered World War I, he immediately joined the Marines, participated in all the bitter fighting of his 5th Regiment, 43rd Company—Mont Blanc, Soissons, Verdun, Belleau Wood—and received almost every award for personal bravery, including a Distinguished Service Cross, Navy Cross, and Croix de guerre. "As a result of wounds I received in action," he wrote in 1932, "I shall never be entirely well again so long as I live"—wounds to the body and to the psyche as well.

Behind him also were the years with Waterman when he was helping to organize the Mobile home office, traveling over the East and Midwest to "solicit freight," and putting three times the money he took out as salary back into the company. Then there were the years in Europe: the depressive atmosphere in Hamburg as he watched Hitler's rise to power (so well depicted in "Personal Letter") and the more pleasant though uneasy days in London from 1935 to 1937 (reflected in "Sweet, Who Was the Armorer's Maid" and "A Short History of England").

Almost all of these experiences had already found some expression in the novels and short stories of these busy years. On trains, in hotels and apartments in little towns and big cities, William March had always found time to read and to write. From the days of his schoolboy interest in composing verse and fiction he had come to know creative writing as a pleasure as well as a sort of necessary therapy. For a decade now he had published with considerable success. His first important story, "The Holly Wreath," had appeared in the October *Forum* of 1929, and using his World War I letter-diary (sent from France to his sister Margaret), he had re-created his war experiences in the powerful novel, *Company K* (1933). The growing to manhood of a boy in south Alabama is the theme of *Come in at the Door* (1934); and while he was working in Germany and England he recalled the environment of Lockhart, Alabama, where, after finishing the only school in town at fourteen, he began to work in the sawmill. This village he had renamed Hodgetown in the novel *The Tallons* (1936)—the dramatic story of two brothers, a farmer and a mill worker, both in love with the same girl.

In addition to these novels, his short stories had appeared in leading magazines and in *The O. Henry Prize Stories* and *The Best American Short Stories*, and *The Little Wife and Other Stories* had been collected in 1935. Now he had a second volume of short stories ready, *Some Like Them Short*. During the 1930's he had also been writing fables. His pithy style, his unending invention of situation, and his concern with the kinks of human behavior all predicted the fabulist. In 1930 he had approached Little, Brown and Company—which was later to issue *Some Like Them Short* (1939) and his most ambitious novel, *The Looking-Glass* (1943)—about the idea of a group of fables, "but they rejected it pleasantly but quite firmly."

The fables venture would not be downed so neatly, however, for the inter-chapter sections of *Come in at the Door* entitled "The Whisperer," which so disturbed the American and British reviewers, were in reality the thoughts of a sort of a cosmic moralist who views the story and the writer of the story from ironic parallels of parable. Later, in the final chapter of *The Looking-Glass,* when the popular novelist Minnie McMinn is asked why she never married Professor St. Joseph, she replies by reading a fable, "The End of the Farmer's Daughter."

"About 1938," then, after he had arranged his second volume of short stories and while he was making plans for his longest and most complex novel, *The Looking-Glass,* William March turned in earnest to his fables. Though he knew they were scarcely what he called "a commercial venture from a publisher's viewpoint," he was now financially free to write as he pleased. A well-healed, middle-aged bachelor of simple tastes, he set about giving full range to his view of the ironic kaleidoscope of this inhumane world.

As a writer of fables, March is distinctly in the tradition of Aesop, or more accurately that of Phaedrus, through whom we know our best Aesop. Unlike George Ade and James Thurber, whose fables are unique and original in style, March adopts a style purposefully flat and folk-like; the sentences, though often quite complex in structure, employ only the simple connectives of the

Bible, *The Pilgrim's Progress,* and fairy tales. March makes almost no experiments with the fable of tone and mood like the young French writer, Anne Bodart; and he is totally apart from the allusive, decorative manner of the poets La Fontaine and Gay. March's fables are strongly didactic; they are sharp and ironic like many of the *Fantastic Fables* of Ambrose Bierce.

On the surface March as a fable writer is a traditionalist, but within the framework of the tradition lies his originality. To the charmingly ambiguous world of Aesop and Phaedrus, where the animals lead a sort of double life of both beasts and human beings, March has added the timeless countries of the Bretts and the Wittins, with kings, queens, bishops and wise men. These lands with their towns of Kafka-like nightmarish implications ("The Strangers," "The Disasters") furnish an urban hinterland for the more rural landscape of the Greek and Roman fabulists.

To make this link with the classic-fable tradition self-evident, March has placed Aesop in the introductory and concluding positions of his arrangement. In the first fable Aesop demonstrates to King Croesus the power of the fable to soften the burdens of new taxes, "since the fable is, and always has been, the platitude's natural frame." Here is a double-barreled warning: these fables are classic in plan, and they underline the platitudes of life. This the reader discovers for himself when he comes upon the pleasant retelling of Aesop's "The Oak and the Reed," transmuted slightly into "The Rigid Oak and the Flexible Reed." In "The Disasters," when a woman hurries to her home only to find her street in chaos, and learning that the Wittins have declared war and are marching forthwith to the borders, she exclaims with relief, "Oh, thank Heaven! For a moment I thought Mama had fallen and hurt her hip again!" The platitude of the small world of *self* is shockingly omnipresent.

Aesop is also in the concluding section of these fables. Using the bare facts of Herodotus and discarding the elaborate "fabrications" of Plutarch and Planudes, March has the Delphians throw Aesop off the cliff not because of the warning of the oracle and not because his wit was too sharp and biting, but because he told fables—nothing but fables—and he was boring. This and the unique stretchable quality of Truth form the *apologia pro fabulis suis.*

The entire collection is distinguished not only for the variety of methods of handling the moral and the balance of dialogue and narration, but also for the rounded whole that gradually forms a way of viewing life from some central cosmography and cosmology. Although the individual fables are detachable and enjoyable in their own rights, the whole is also meaningful, and the individual parts of this whole take on a new significance as one reads the entire collection in the author's ordering.

When, for example, one reads of the death of Aesop in "Aesop's Last Fable," he is wryly amused; but when he reads this account in sequence, he remembers the over-confidence of Croesus' adviser and modifies his amusement to something approaching cosmic justice. The next fable, however, "Iadmon and Aesop," transfigures this concept of retributive justice toward one of sympathy for the man of letters because he is usually misjudged, until he is safely dead, not only by the world at large (the Delphians), but also by his own family (Iadmon). Or to take another example, when in "The Farmhand and His Judges" the convicted laborer exclaims, after describing his attitude toward squirrels, that he would prefer to be judged by a jury of squirrels than by one of his peers "with their own terrifying ignorance," the reader understands the farmhand's position, for he remembers from "The Squirrel and the Trees" how squirrels, though "forgetful and foolish," are the planters of "life-giving trees," capable of empathizing man's search for beauty (the box of colored crayons).

However unique the ordering and linking of a collection of fables, the basic merit of the work must always lie in the individual fables. Every reader will find a few here that he does not particularly like and others that are immediate favorites, but most often he will say "How true, how painfully true!" And this will be his accolade for William March, since the fable and life itself are platitude; March's view of the world is a hard one, ruled by logic, irony, and pain.

The *99 Fables* takes on a special significance after

the death of the author. Because of an insistent iteration of certain "platitudes" and because March revised them over a period of twenty years, the fables form a sort of writer's notebook of ideas—the writer whom Alistair Cooke has called "the most underrated of all contemporary American writers of fiction." William March was not a prolific letter writer; in fact, one of his close friends referred to him as being "niggardly of letters." And his only diary—that of World War I—has been destroyed. The fables, then, come close to providing as personal a summary of March's world as we are likely to have. Here are all his favorite ideas, the epitomes of the themes of his fiction.

"The King and the Bright Young Men" and "The King and the Outcast" point up the senseless cruelty that lies at the heart of *Company K*. "The Dog and Her Rival" concludes with "Love can be the most dreadful disguise that hate assumes." This is the tragedy of *The Tallons;* this (along with "The Criminal Female") is the germinating idea for *The Bad Seed* (1954), anticipating the sentence from a letter written in the last year of March's life: ". . . all the major crimes are committed in the name of love." "Wild Horses" grows out of March's horror at watching the Germans gradually give up their liberty, and it also forms the ironic core of "Runagate Niggers," a story that appeared in *Esquire* in 1938. "The Fat Woman and the Terrier" ends with the dog's asking, "Why did they destroy my one reason for living?" This need for a life illusion is the theme of *The Looking-Glass*. And his next novel, *October Island* (1952), March's attack on militant Christianity, is foreshadowed in three fables: "The World and Its Redeemers," "The Prophets and the Mountains," and "The Miracle." Even the recurrent sanity of March's world— that of unthinking women who raise children or run boarding houses, of prostitutes and Negroes—is dramatized in these fables by "the creatures of the underbrush." When the last of the Bretts runs frantically from battle and announces that this is the end of the world and that he is the last of living creatures, the tiny animals of the brush reply, "Excuse us for doubting your word, but in this field alone there are, at this moment, millions of creatures alive and breathing and leading their normal lives." They endure because they are unashamed of their fear and because they are "so much easier to amuse than the general reader."

When March finished the first complete version of the fables in 1938, there were "about 125." He discarded all but ninety-nine during the forties as he re-worked them and published about forty-five in various "little magazines" and New York newspapers. A few years before his death, about the time he was moving to New Orleans and buying in the French Quarter the first house he ever owned, he went through all his papers and rediscovered his book of fables. He found them "too good to destroy," so he reworked them once again. The text that follows is chiefly taken from this last revision, but in a few instances the earlier versions have been employed where the phrasing seems indisputably superior. The accompanying illustrations have been designed and executed for this edition by Richard Brough, distinguished artist and member of the art faculty, University of Alabama. Because William March himself was an astute critic of art and a possessor of one of the most valuable private collections of modern French masterpieces in the United States, it is our hope that these sketches would have pleased this Aesop of the Lost Generation.

William T. Going
Alton, Illinois

March, 1959.

99 fables by
william march

1

aesop and king croesus

KING CROESUS DECIDED TO
put heavier taxes on his people who were even then sullen and discontented with the burdens they already bore, and he discussed the matter with his trusted messenger, the slave Aesop. Aesop could find no flaw in the king's reasoning, but if Croesus put the matter so bluntly to his subjects, he feared there would be barricades and bloodshed—a situation which could be avoided if Croesus would permit him, Aesop, to break the bad news in a fable.

This was agreed upon, and later Aesop spoke to the assembled people: "The lion decided to take even heavier tribute from his subjects, and as a result there was anger among them, some of them advocating an open rebellion, but the wise fox said, 'What can we gain by desperate measures? If we depose the lion, whose greedy ways we at least understand, we may find ourselves with a tyrant worse than he is; if we lose, we may have taken from us the little we now have. Isn't it wiser, therefore, to endure the evils we are familiar with than to invite strange evils of which we know nothing?' "

When Aesop finished, the people wept and went away, accepting their new burdens as something that could not be avoided, since the fable is, and always has been, the platitude's natural frame.

2

the insulted rabbit

A FARMER CAME TO THE edge of the forest and scolded the animals that were loitering there. He said, "No sooner is my back turned than you sneak under my fence and eat my cabbages!" In turn, he pointed at the wolf, the lion, the panther, and the tiger, but those animals laughed and said, "We're meat eaters. What you're looking for is a cabbage eater."

Then the farmer pointed at the rabbit and said, "It wouldn't surprise me if you knew about this, too."

The rabbit thumped the ground with his leg, advanced a step or two in the farmer's direction, and said, "Don't you dare insult me! Don't you dare call me a cabbage eater!"

A creature is insulted only when he agrees with his accuser.

[3]

3

the escaped elephant

AFTER SOME YEARS IN A circus, an elephant escaped and returned to her jungle. As she waded into the river and took her old place there, her friends asked what her life had been like in the years of her absence. "I suppose they starved you and made you do work beyond your strength," said an old bull.

The escaped elephant said, "No, it wasn't that way at all. I got better food with the circus than I ever got for myself at home; and the only work I did was walk in the parade, balance on a ball, and beat a drum in the tent. Everybody was nice to me, especially a man named

Tommy who took care of me. . . . Poor little Tommy! He was so sweet and silly. He used to tie a pink bow on my tail, and once he painted my toenails yellow and reddened my trunk with chalk, threatening to walk me in the parade that way if I didn't behave better and eat my hay. Well, we laughed that time until our sides ached.

"It was because they made so much noise," said the escaped elephant. "They were forever playing brass bands, shouting at one another, and firing off cannons for no reason at all. Men are strong enough to stand that din and confusion, but I'm not." She turned in her tracks, splashing the warm, muddy water over her hide. "The truth of the matter is," she said, "that I'm just too thin-skinned."

4

the persimmon tree

A POSSUM WATCHED THE persimmons on the fox's tree turn from green to yellow to a tantalizing shade of gold. "How pleasant it would be if I could eat my fill of the ripe fruit," he said. He turned away, regretting that his moral code prevented his shaking the tree and taking what he wanted. "No," he said. "The fox is my friend and benefactor, and he trusts me. Oh, no!"

[6]

And so things went for several days, and then the first frost fell. That day the persimmons had reached their finest flavor, and as the possum stared up at the purple-and-silver fruit, his mouth watered; but he turned away finally and went back home. He found his wife outside in the sunlight, and as he came closer, she sniffed the frosty air and said, "What a morning this would be for eating persimmons! When I think how sweet they are at this moment—so fragrant, so juicy, so wrinkled at their edges by the frost—I could break down and cry my eyes out."

The possum stopped short and said, "That settles it. I'll take those persimmons if it's the last thing I ever do. . . . Why, what sort of a creature would I be if I deprived my sweet, faithful wife of persimmons—endangering her health and making her cry her dear eyes out."

We often do for the sake of others what we would like to do for ourselves.

5

the young poet and the worm

A YOUNG POET STOOD BY A
riverbank and looked at the world about him. It was
summer and the countryside was green; fruit hung in the
orchards, cattle ate in the meadows of white clover, and
the yellow grain waved and ripened in the fields. It was
then the poet knew how greatly God had honored mankind and with what abundant and varied gifts, and
overcome with emotion he cried out, "How beautiful,
how wide, how splendid is the world—this rich, perfect
world which God created for man's pleasure!"

An earthworm listened to the poet's words, appraising his plump, pink body. He said, "Perhaps the perfection of the world was made for the pleasure of man, as you think. I don't know about that, but there's one thing I do know from my own experience: the perfection of man was assuredly made for the pleasure of worms."

6

the bird and the waterfall

A BIRD OF PARADISE BUILT
his nest near a waterfall. The animals of the forest came
often to look at the fall and admire its beautiful colors,
for when the sun shone on it, it was like a brilliantly
tinted rainbow. The bird of paradise, when visitors
arrived, would strut and preen himself, lifting his tail

[10]

and spreading his wings so that his iridescence could be seen by all, but the visitors paid him little attention. When they noticed him at all, they only said, "Look at that poor drab bird. How pale he seems against the background of a rainbow."

If you would exhibit your talents to advantage, it's wise to find the appropriate background for them.

7

the criminal female

to try some female offenders. The first was a squirrel who
had stolen the food supply of her sister. "It's true! It's
all true!" said the squirrel; "but it was a cold, hard
winter, and I was thin, and my lover likes fat squirrels.
I stole my sister's food only that I might become plump
and desirable, and thus win back the love of my sweetheart. It was love and love alone that made me do it."

The jury nodded in sympathy, and the judge released
the squirrel who had made herself so fat and seductive.

The next was a leopardess, and hardly had she taken
the stand before she said, "It's true I killed the dear

husband that I loved so well, but I did it only for his own good: you see, he was leaving me for a younger leopardess, and I knew he couldn't be happy with her, having once known my love, so to spare him pain, I killed him."

The jury said not guilty, and the judge agreed.

The third offender, a lioness, was accused of selling her cubs to a hunter. She admitted her offense, as her sisters had done, and the judge said, "You sold your cubs because you loved them so greatly, didn't you, madam?"

"Well, no," said the lioness. "I sold my cubs because it was to my advantage to do that. You see, the hunter offered me such a large sum for them that I'd have been a fool not to have taken it."

When the judge could speak at all, he cried out: "You are a disgrace to your sex, and you deserve the death sentence I'm going to impose on you!"

Any crime is permitted a female if she remembers to do it in the name of love.

8

the sheep and the soldiers

A COMPANY OF HIGH-spirited soldiers on their way to the wars fell out to rest beside a country lane, and before them were sheep browsing on the side of a hill. The sheep moved with lowered eyes, following their leader wherever he led them and bumping their faces against the rumps of the sheep in front of them when he stopped suddenly or changed direction. Seeing the sheep, the soldiers laughed boisterously, capered about, and slapped one another on the back.

The sheep looked up at the sound of the merriment and stared back at the soldiers; then their leader said, "Why do you laugh at us? We, at least, know what we are and what our end will be."

At once the soldiers rushed to the fence and hurled stones at the sheep, since a comedian finds everything amusing except a joke on himself.

9

the stableboy

A STABLEBOY IN THE
provinces had one ambition, and that was to go to court
and learn to be a gentleman: for this reason he saved his
wages, hoping his ambition would be realized in time.
One of the grooms had been in the capital when he was
younger, and had stories to tell of the fine gentlemen he
had seen there, describing their dress, their refinements,
and their delicate manners.

And so things went, while the stableboy's savings grew
with the passing months, and then he got a letter from
his brother who lived nearby. The brother explained

that he'd been sick, and since he had not been able to work, his family was in want. He begged the stableboy to send them money to help them along.

"Tell him no," said the old groom. "Explain that you need the money for yourself."

"That would be selfish, and it would hurt his feelings, too. I wouldn't want to do anything that mean."

"Then say you haven't got any money. He won't know the difference."

"That would be a lie," said the stableboy after a pause. "I couldn't do a thing like that."

That day he sent his brother all the money he had saved and began all over again; but hardly a month had passed before news came of the brother's death. He had left a widow and five small children, and nothing else; and his widow implored her brother-in-law to come take over the farm and work it, for without a man on the place to look out for them, she feared they'd starve before the winter was over. This was the last thing the stableboy had counted on, and he went to the barn to think matters out.

The old groom came up, and being told of the situation, he said, "If you do it, you'll have a lifetime job on your hands raising those children. You'll never get to court."

"I know that," said the stableboy sadly, "but what else can I possibly do? I'll just have to resign myself to the fact that I'll never be a gentleman."

10

the world and its redeemers

goats had lived in comfort, each generation finding itself better off than its predecessor. In time they might have achieved contentment, but when things seemed most stable with them, a redeemer appeared, saying it was the destiny of mountain goats to convert and enlighten the world. The goats, aroused by the zeal of the prophet, started a war against their neighbors, but to their amazement these neighbors neither knew they were lost nor desired to be saved, and resisted with all their strength, and the final result, after years of destruction, was that both sides were almost annihilated.

In the end, the mountain goats were driven back to their own country, but things had gone to ruin during their absence. The paths they had made were forgotten, their dwellings had fallen down, and the fields where they had grazed were covered with nettles; in fact, the goats who had managed to survive found themselves once more in the darkness, the poverty, and the despair from which their ancestors had so patiently emerged.

The world could have been saved long ago if it had not been for its redeemers.

11

the donkey and the calf

A BULL WHO FOUND IT necessary to make a long journey was concerned about his son, a calf too young to undertake the trip on foot. As a result, he offered to pay the donkey if he would carry the calf on his back, and the donkey, seeing how light the calf was, agreed, well pleased with the bargain he had made.

For some days the donkey trotted along, hardly aware of the load he was carrying, but as the weeks went by, and the calf grew bigger and bigger, he found himself straining under a load so heavy that it was intolerable. At last he told his employer that he could go no farther, begging to be released from his contract, but the bull refused. That day the donkey staggered forward as best he could, but toward nightfall his legs collapsed and he fell to the earth, crushed by the weight of the lusty, full-grown bull he was bearing.

Carry a calf, and you'll wind up with a bull on your back.

12

white and yellow corn

A FARMER FED HIS CHICKENS
on white corn which he grew in his own fields. One year
he decided to plant yellow corn instead of white corn, but
when the yellow corn was harvested, his chickens refused
to eat it. The situation soon became serious, and it was
plain the chickens would starve if something were not
done. It was then the farmer hit on a scheme, and he
told his wife and children to go to the barnyard and
follow the instructions he had previously given them.

[22]

This they did, and when the farmer began scattering the yellow corn, his family got down on their hands and knees and gobbled it up, cackling, flapping their arms, pecking and shoving one another out of the way. Instantly the fowls came running up, stretching their necks forward and snapping up the yellow corn as fast as they could.

When the hens had eaten all they could hold, the farmer said, "Well, we've learned one thing today: if you want to convince a fool, you must do so in the language he understands."

13

the two stags

WHILE THE REMAINDER
of the herd were resting in the glade, a stag with a fine
spread of antlers would stand on top of a hill and scan the
horizon, looking for a fight. One day he saw a stag whose
antlers were as fine as his own, and the warlike stag ran
toward him, pawing the earth. The stranger braced
himself and met the charge head-on. They fought for an
hour, and by that time their antlers were so interlocked
that there was no way of separating them.

When the two stags were exhausted, they fell to the earth. They lay that way for many days, dying in the sight of plenty, while the remainder of the herd browsed in the meadows or slept in the glade.

Make hatred your business and you guarantee your own destruction.

14

the crow and the parrot

A PARROT, MUCH PRIZED by his mistress, struck up a friendship with a crow. One day the parrot's mistress came to the window to see how her pet was getting along, and the crow hid behind some vines. "Does my pretty polly like the nice sun?" she asked in a mincing voice.

"Does my pretty polly like the nice sun?" echoed the parrot in the same tone his mistress had used.

The woman pursed her lips and made a kissing noise. Instantly the parrot duplicated the sound so perfectly that it would have been impossible to tell which had been made by the mistress and which by her pet. The woman laughed with pleasure, and said, "Oh, you are so clever, my dear! You are so *clever!*"

The parrot's mood changed with her own. He, too, laughed and said, "Oh, you are so clever, my dear! You are so *clever!*"

When the mistress had gone, the crow said, "You have no opinions of your own, my friend. All you do is duplicate what your mistress says."

The parrot said, "That's correct; I can't deny it."

"It seems to me she'd be so sick of hearing her words echoed that she'd long since have pulled out your feathers in boredom or wrung your neck in a rage," said the crow.

The parrot said, "No bird that lives gets the love and honor that I get. Can you name another creature who's reached the age of sixty without hearing a single cross word?"

15

the mongoose and the cobra

THE MONGOOSE AND COBRA were enemies, sworn to destroy each other on sight. One day the mongoose met a holy man, and after hearing his views on brotherhood and love, he said he would put things right between himself and the cobra before the sun went down that day; but the cobra, when he saw his enemy approaching, reared in his nest, hissed, and flicked his tongue.

The mongoose was not alarmed. He told of his talk with the holy man, and to prove his new viewpoint, he walked boldly into the cobra's den. He said, "See, I've forgiven the crimes that you and your kind have inflicted on mongooses."

At that instant the cobra fixed his fangs in the throat of the mongoose. "The fact that you have forgiven me is no reason for you to assume that I have stopped hating you," he said.

16

the wasp and the caterpillar

THE FEMALE WASP, WHEN she found the caterpillar she was looking for, pierced his nerve center and carried him off to the nest she had prepared. The male wasp turned to the beetle and said, "The caterpillar isn't really dead; he's only paralyzed. If my wife killed him outright, he'd quickly rot; but with things the way they are, he'll last until the eggs my wife is depositing around him have hatched, and our

[30]

young will thus have fresh meat to feed on until they can take care of themselves." He waited a moment and then went on, "How beautiful is love! How tender! How compassionate!"

The caterpillar looked up at that moment and said, "It may seem that way to a wasp, but I don't think many caterpillars will agree with you."

17

nightingales and
mockingbirds

A MERCHANT IMPORTED A
pair of nightingales and had an enclosed garden built for
them. Afterwards, he and his friends would sit patiently,
waiting for the birds to sing their song; but if nightingales were a rarity in this country, mockingbirds were
found everywhere, and after the garden was finished, they
gathered outside in great numbers.

Now, it is well known that the mockingbirds can duplicate any song in the world, and after they had listened to the notes of the nightingales, they mastered that song too, and, pleased with its novelty, they sang it at all hours of the day and night; but nobody—least of all the rich merchant and his friends—listened to the commonplace mockingbirds: they went to the enclosed garden as before, waiting patiently until the captive birds relented and sang a few unwilling bars.

Those too eager to display their talents are seldom appreciated.

18

the farmer and the mink

A FARMER CAUGHT THE mink who was raiding his chicken roost and brought him to trial. The mink, acting in his own defense, asked that the indictment be read to him, and the judge said, "You are charged with destroying the farmer's hens. How do you plead?"

[34]

The mink said, "I plead innocent, for I have not destroyed the farmer's hens, as he maintains." He pointed to the six fat pullets that lay on the table as evidence. "The farmer has accused me of destroying his hens," he went on, "and yet he offers in evidence, to make a case against me, the very hens he charges me with having destroyed."

The judge nodded, and the mink continued rapidly: "To sum up, it seems to me the farmer's case comes to this: if I *destroyed* his hens, as he charges, then he has no evidence against me since the evidence, being destroyed, no longer exists; if, on the other hand, the evidence I am said to have destroyed is *still* in existence, then obviously I could not have *destroyed* it, and I am innocent."

The judge, impressed by the mink's reasoning, dismissed the case.

At once the farmer got up in protest. "But everybody knows the mink destroyed my hens!" he said. "I came into court seeking justice. Everybody knows I have not received it."

The judge said: "This court isn't interested in what you're saying. Our concern here is to administer the law."

19

the farmer boy and the ladies

A FARMER BOY AT THE fair paid his money and went into the juggler's tent; but he wasn't able to enjoy the show after all, for in front of him were two ladies wearing hats in the latest fashion. The hat of the lady on his right was a full-rigged ship riding atop her piled-up hair, while the hat of the lady on his left was like a pagoda, with one tier rising up from the next, the whole being draped in veiling and topped with a halo of bells.

The farmer boy twisted from side to side, but try as he would, he was not able to see around or above the hats of the fine ladies. He gave up finally and settled back in his chair, and it was then he remembered he had bought a bagful of almonds to eat on his way home. He took out two and cracked them together, but at the sound the ladies flinched and put their hands to their ears, saying coldly over their shoulders, "Some people have no breeding, no manners!—No consideration for the comfort of others!"

20

the proud queen

THERE WAS ONCE A QUEEN so proud that never in her life had she put her foot on the ground. When she got out of her carriage, slaves unrolled a carpet for her to walk on, and as she progressed from her coach to the palace door, ladies-in-waiting walked beside her with screens and fans to see that no dirt touched her.

As she grew older, the queen became more and more arrogant, and as her pride increased, her hatred of dirt grew with it. In her old age, she spent the whole day changing her robes, bathing and perfuming herself, and if a serving woman used words like *clay*, or *dust*, or *earth* in her hearing, she would weep or fly into a rage, crying that such words were unfit for the ears of a great queen.

But the Earth himself drowsed and waited his time, thinking: "The little queen well knows that some day she, too, will be dust, and that is why she is so proud now, for pride is only a denial of what we know in our hearts is true."

21

the truthful hawk

A COMMUNITY OF BEES were raided so often by the bear that they found another home for themselves, and they offered the hawk a reward to move their honey for them, provided he took an oath not to mention the new location to the bear. The hawk agreed, took the oath, made the transfer, and pocketed his reward.

Later, the bear asked him where the bees had gone, but the hawk said, "I can't tell you. I took an oath not to mention the location of the new hive." But when the bear offered him a reward greater than the one the bees had given him, the hawk saw a way out of the dilemma, and he said, "I swore I would not mention the location to you. That was the oath I took, and naturally I will not *mention* it."

At that he rose from the ground and flew slowly away, looking back now and then to see that the bear was following him. When the bear knew the location of the new hive, he paid the reward he had offered the hawk for breaking his oath.

"I did not break my oath," said the indignant hawk. "I observed my oath to the letter, and I defy anybody to prove differently."

Liars often conform strictly to the truth.

22

the polecat and his friends

A POLECAT WAS INDIGNANT at the way the other animals treated him. He told his grievances to the old tortoise, and as he recalled the slights he suffered, his voice trembled. He said, "Do they ask me to their parties? Do they come when I invite them to mine? That never happens, I assure you. They even back off into the bushes when they see me on the road. They think they're better than I am, that's what! They're all undemocratic snobs!"

The old tortoise listened for a time and then said, "Perhaps so, but there could be another reason for their conduct, you know."

"What?" asked the polecat. "What other explanation is there?"

"Well, after all, you do stink a little," said the old tortoise mildly.

23

the democratic bretts

THE WITTINS, HEARING THEIR neighbors the Bretts had a new form of government, sent a party to study the system and report on how it worked out in practice. The delegation found the Bretts anxious to enlighten others. "Our system is simple," they said. "It's founded on the belief that every man is the equal of every other."

[44]

The Wittins asked, "Do you believe you are the equal of our king, whose ancestors, as everybody knows, were the Sun and the Moon?"

The Bretts answered loudly, "We are the equal of your king in every way. There's no such thing as one man being higher than another."

The Wittins glanced at one another in astonishment and then said: "In our country there is a murderer so depraved that he is incapable of feeling those human emotions that distinguish some men from beasts. Now, if all men are equal, and you are as high as a divinely born king, are you also as low as a monster?"

Everyone is as good as the best, but no one is as bad as the worst.

24

the distinguished and
the obscure

ON A REMOTE PLAIN,
between a mountain and a river, many animals lived,
safe from the habits of humans. There was a variety of
animals on the plain, and they differed widely as to size,
strength, and brilliance of coloration. The small, dull-
colored animals, such as the field mice and hedgehog,
lived obscurely in the bush or in burrows in the ground,
venturing out only when they needed food, and blending
even then so unobtrusively with their backgrounds that
they could hardly be seen by the sharpest eye.

[46]

Things went quietly for some years, and then a party of hunters invaded the plain with nets and guns. Within a few days the large, imposing animals, since there was no way to hide their brilliance, were all killed, being betrayed in this crisis by their very distinction and importance; but the small, trivial creatures, safe in their tunnels and burrows, hardly realized what was going on above their heads. They went about their affairs as usual, the routine of their lives being merely disturbed a little; then, when the hunters had gone away, they came out of their burrows, seeing no changes of importance and taking up once more their placid, changeless existences.

The obscure escape and remain forever the same.

25

the magician and the peasants

A MAGICIAN FELL OUT with his assistant, a man who had long since learned the secrets of his master. The assistant, wanting revenge, waited until the magician performed next at a fair. In the middle of the act, he stepped forward and explained how the trick was done, stating that the magician had

[48]

none of the powers he claimed, that he was a man like themselves with a few tricks in his bag, tricks which any one of them could learn too, if he put his mind to it. When he had finished, he pointed to the magician and said, "This man has tricked you and defrauded you of your money. If you give him a flogging, you'll be giving him what he's earned a dozen times over."

But the people did not vent their anger on the magician who had deluded them so pleasantly and had given them so much to talk about during the long winter months; they turned instead on the assistant who had shown them up as fools, and in a moment he was running for his life, pursued by a mob of angry, shouting peasants.

26

the kissless lovebird

A LOVEBIRD BECAME disgusted with the habits of her kind. She eyed the love-making of her sisters with disdain, and often would cry out angrily: "What silly lives you lead!—Kissing, cooing, and sitting cheek-to-cheek! What do you see in it?"

One day the kissless lovebird flew farther into the jungle than usual, and there she met a strange lovebird who took a fancy to her. At once the kissless lovebird stated her views, but the male bird seemed not to hear her, and at length, alarmed by his activities, she flew toward home as fast as she could, but, as it turned out later, she had waited too long and the male overtook her when she was only halfway home. When at last she was safe in her nest once more, her sisters gathered to console her. They said, "We know your high standards. We realize what a dreadful experience this has been for you."

At that the lovebird wept and said, "My tragedy is not that I found love a terrible experience, as I had thought, but that I didn't."

27

the widow and her son

A RICH WIDOW DISCOVERED her young son was missing, and although a search was made, he was not found. Later, a report came that the boy had been seen playing near a horse traders' camp, and the mother went to that place too, but the band had gone. Afterwards, she spent her time trying to trace the child, but her efforts came to nothing, and finally she set out herself, asking everyone she met on the road if he had seen a pink-cheeked, five-year-old boy with yellow hair.

In the years that followed, the widow grew older and more bent, but she kept up her search; then, one day, she rested in a village far from her native land, and asked her question once more. This time the woman to whom she spoke said quickly, "Did all this happen years ago? Did your son go away with some horse traders? . . . The boy I'm thinking about crawled into one of the wagons and went to sleep. I know, because I took care of him for a long time."

She led the widow to a camp beyond the town. She paused when she came to a bearded, thickset man who was feeding pigs almost as dirty as himself. He looked up when he saw the two women, spat, and grinned foolishly. The widow covered her eyes and cried, saying, "How can you be so cruel as to lie to me? How can you say this is my child, when my son is a little boy with pink cheeks and curls?"

She turned and walked down the road, but stopping at every farmhouse and tavern to ask her identical, unending question.

28

the wild horses

A HERD OF WILD HORSES who had roamed the plains found themselves trapped and captured and led away to serve the purposes of men. While they had been free to go where they chose, to do what suited them best at all times, they had not thought about themselves or the happiness of their lot, accepting their blessings as things to be expected; but when they found themselves in a corral with bits in their mouths and hobbles on their legs, they were alarmed and huddled together. "We will not submit to this injustice," they said. "Liberty is a beautiful and precious thing, and we must not lose it."

An old field horse stood beside the corral and said, "I was caught young. I've seen many wild horses brought to the corral you're in now. I've heard them all say the things you're saying, but if you'll lift your heads and

[54]

look about you, you'll see them all working for the comfort of our master." He sighed, shook out his mane, and continued, "When we realize how precious our liberty is and swear to preserve it, it is too late, for already we have lost it."

29

the elephants
and the antelopes

FOR A LONG TIME THE antelopes and the elephants had lived without conflict, and then the antelopes became conscious of their comparative weakness. They said to one another: "Even though we are at peace with the elephants, and hope always to be, we must strengthen our position, in case the attack, which we have no reason to expect, should come."

[56]

Thereupon they posted sentries and went about, not singly as before, but in wedge-shaped formations of tens and twelves. The elephants, puzzled by the change in the antelopes' behavior, asked the reason for it. The antelopes explained their position. "But why?" asked the elephants. "Have we injured you in the past in any way?"

"No," said the antelopes; "it's only that we want to be prepared for disaster if, by chance, it should come."

The elephants, still puzzled, consulted together, and from that day on the relationship between the elephants and the antelopes became more and more strained. At last the elephants got so they would stare suspiciously at the antelopes or turn aside in order to avoid them. "You see?" said the antelopes. "It's working out just as we thought." And so things got worse and worse until the antelopes, really frightened now, began building barricades and pits.

The elephants massed at the edge of the jungle to watch; then, stampeding in panic, they charged the antelopes' defenses and destroyed them, driving the antelopes who had survived back into the forest.

Those who expect disaster are rarely disappointed.

30

the rigid oak and the flexible reed

AN OAK TREE GREW BESIDE a stream, and although he was proud of his power and spread of branches, he did condescend to talk to a reed nearby, a thing so flexible that he would bend if even a dragonfly lit on his stalk. Seeing this, the oak would say, "Keep your head up! Carry yourself as I do!"

And so things went until a hurricane struck one day. The reed at the first blast trembled and fell flat against the earth. He looked up after a time to see how the oak was faring, and it was then he knew that the oak at last had met a thing stronger than himself. "Bend down!" said the little reed. "Bend down if you want to escape!"

But the inflexible oak could not take the reed's advice,

since he had never learned to bend. He knew but one
way to meet ill fortune, and that was to resist with all his
strength, and he held himself more and more stiffly
against the wind; but his firmness helped him little this
time, and soon his branches were torn away, and his
trunk began to split. "Bend down!" said the reed. "Bend
down if you want to escape!"

Then, even as he called out, he saw the oak uprooted
and hurled across the field, but when the hurricane had
blown itself out, the reed began to rise from his place on
the ground until after a time he was standing as erect as
before, ready to bend in any direction in the face of any
adverse wind.

31

the king and his successor

A KING, DESIRING AN HEIR
as wise and well-informed as himself, hit on a test to
settle the matter. In his childhood he had visited a foreign country where he had seen a monkey; now in his old
age he determined to ask the contenders for the throne
what a monkey was, determining in this way both their
learning and experience.

One by one the contenders came before him, each defining a monkey as best he could, but in the end the king said they had all failed. "These men I've examined are the best informed in my kingdom," he said, "and yet not one of them knows what a monkey is."

One of the court slaves spoke up: "I know what a monkey is. As a boy at home I saw them in the streets every day: a monkey is a small animal in a red coat who wears a cocked hat with a feather in it, and turns a handspring after he picks up the coin you toss him."

The king said, "This boy shall be my successor, for he's the only one I've found wise enough to rule over you."

32

the gull and the earthquake

A SEAGULL, TIRED FROM A long flight over the ocean, flew toward land and lighted on a crag, but, as it happened, an earthquake occurred at that identical moment, and the shoreline trembled, lifted upward, and collapsed beneath him. At this, the gull flew back to sea, screaming tragically, "See what I've done: I lighted on the crag to rest, and I wrecked the entire coast!"

His companions consoled him as best they could. "I wouldn't take all the blame," they said. "There was an earthquake, too."

[62]

33

the shepherd
and his monument

WHEN THE WITTINS DECIDED
to erect a monument to the hero who founded their
nation, the sculptor was faced with a problem: where to
find a model whose body was as godlike as the hero's was
said to have been. For months the search went on, and
then at last the perfect model was found. He was a

[63]

young shepherd, and they brought him to the capital, where the court made a great fuss over him during the months the sculptor was at work; then, when the statue was finished, and the marble unveiled to the public, the shepherd feasted for a week, even appearing in public with the king himself; but later, after he had served his purpose, he went back to his village in the mountains again, and from that time on the shepherd talked of nothing except the great honor that had been shown him, and the people of his village listened to the story he told over and over.

Toward the end of his life, he wanted to see the statue once more before he died. He set out on foot, and he arrived at the capital weeks later; but his peasant clothes were in tatters by that time, and his white beard soiled and matted. He found the monument there in the great park, and stood looking at it. He stared so long and so earnestly that a crowd gathered about him. "What's the matter, old man?" they asked. "Have you lost something?"

"I was the model for that statue," said the old shepherd. "The king who reigned long before the present one was born sent out messengers, and of all the young men in the country I was chosen."

The crowd laughed at the tottering, foolish old man, and he turned in surprise. "You doubt me?" he asked; and when the people continued to laugh and wink at one another, he dropped his cloak and stood before them naked, in the exact pose he had once taken for the sculptor. "Then see for yourselves!" he cried triumphantly. At this the crowd laughed louder than before, and when the shepherd asked the reason, they said, "Look in the fountain, old man!"

The shepherd came closer to the monument and examined his reflection in the water; then, glancing again at the heroic figure above him, he put on his cloak and walked away.

34

the ditch

A RABBIT WHO HAD BEEN sent out to examine the premises of a farmer recited his findings upon his return. When he had finished, the raccoon spoke: "How wide did you say that ditch around the peanut patch is?"

"About four feet."

"You said three and a half feet the first time."

"What difference does it make?—Four feet, three and a half feet. It's the same thing."

The raccoon said: "It may be the same thing to you, since you can leap both high and wide, but to a raccoon, who can jump three and a half feet, but not four, it's the difference between life and death."

35

the old cow and the heifers

A HERD OF CATTLE WERE told that on the other side of the mountain there were fields so green that they could browse all day on the sweetest clover. They set out for their paradise in excellent spirits, telling one another that their troubles were now at an end. Only one cautious old cow took no part in the merrymaking. "Maybe it's all they say it is, and then maybe it isn't," she said.

A couple of young heifers turned on her and said, "At least let us have the pleasure of believing in such a place until we know different."

"When you heifers are as old as I am, you'll find out it's better to be surprised than disappointed," said the old cow sadly.

[67]

36

the bees' honey

THE BEES, HAVING MADE their honey, were beset by their enemies, the farmer and the bear. The bear claimed the honey because the tree in which the bees had their hive was on his land; the farmer said the honey was his because the clover that produced it had grown in his meadow; and so, caught between two claimants, the bees went to the lion for protection.

[68]

The lion, afraid to offend either the farmer, who could easily trap him in a pitfall, or the bear, with whom he had a hunting arrangement, said, "Since the claims of both sides are equally just, the equitable settlement is to give half to each."

"What about us?" asked the bees. "We worked all summer to make the honey. How can we live this winter without it?"

"You'll have the comb to nibble on," said the lion fairly, "and your natural industry with which to replace what you've lost."

It's easy to be impartial about other people's property.

37

the two seals

AN OLD BULL SEAL FELL
in love with a giddy young female, and for a time the
courtship progressed normally; then the young female
ended the affair abruptly, and said in explanation: "Last
week I had a birthday, and he wanted to give me a present, so I told him to use his own judgment: and what do
you think the old bull selected for me?—A handful of
bright pebbles to play with and a colored ball to bounce

on my nose. I'm afraid to marry him. You could hardly expect a creature whose mind is so immature to care for a wife and family properly."

One of the other seals spoke reassuringly: "I wouldn't be too hard on the old bull. Maybe the presents he selected for you don't indicate the quality of his mind so much as they do his opinion of the quality of yours."

38

the beaver's house

A BEAVER HAD FINISHED
a house of which he was proud, and he invited his friend
the eagle to look at it. He said that although he considered the new structure the most perfect he had ever
seen, he realized his opinion might be a little prejudiced,
and he asked the eagle to say frankly what he thought
of the new house, as it was only thus that he could learn
to correct his faults and build even better houses in the
future.

The eagle, deceived by his friend's modesty and earnestness, said, "It's as good as most houses of its kind, I suppose. It probably seems impressive to you from where you are standing, but if you could examine it from above, you'd see that it's full of flaws, that it isn't well proportioned, and that there are sticks and patches of mud that stick out and give it a crude appearance."

"Thank you for being so completely frank!" said the beaver. "I know, now, that you are truly my friend!"

He went into his dwelling, slamming the door behind him angrily, while the eagle fanned the air with his wings and thought, "Whoever criticizes a friend's work makes an enemy needlessly."

39

the peacock and his bride

A TURKEY HEN FELL IN love with a peacock, and afterwards she would watch while he strutted in a circle. If occasionally he accepted the food she scratched up for him or acknowledged her existence with a glance, she was so faint with pleasure that she would run back of the barn and lie down. Each day the peacock would perform for the hen's pleasure, letting her admire him to her heart's content, and then one day he suggested that they get married.

The drab little hen was overcome at her good fortune. She agreed meekly, and they went that day to the owl to have the ceremony performed. The owl, seeing the great difference in their coloration and temperaments, was doubtful that such a union was wise, since they had so little in common on which to build a marriage. The peacock said, "Don't talk silly. We have everything in common for a successful marriage."

"But what?" asked the owl. "What is it you have in common that escapes my eye?"

"Just this," said the peacock, erecting his magnificent tail and strutting in a circle before his hen: "My sweetheart and I both think I'm the most wonderful creature in the wide world, and we both love me to distraction."

40

the grasshoppers and their wealthy neighbors

THE GRASSHOPPERS, SEEING that their neighbors lived in comfort during the hard winter months, called a meeting to discuss conditions. They said the fruits of the earth belonged to all alike, and they proposed, therefore, that the supplies the other animals had gathered be put into a common fund for the benefit of all.

The bees, ants, and squirrels said the plan seemed both sensible and just, and at once furnished a list of the things they had stored up; but before finally agreeing to the plan, they wanted to know what the grasshoppers themselves were going to contribute.

The grasshoppers looked at their wealthy neighbors in astonishment and said, "But we have nothing at all. We thought that was understood when we made our proposal."

Those who have nothing are anxious to share it.

41

the monkey hill

A TROOP OF MONKEYS made their home on a rocky hill, and it seemed a more quarrelsome community never existed, for they had lasting and intricate feuds among themselves, and their dislike of one another was so great it was a mystery they lived together at all. At different times the other animals tried to make peace among the monkeys, but as if the very thought angered them unbearably, they shrieked and chattered worse than before, hurling things at one another so furiously that the mediators retreated in haste.

And so things went, and then a tiger came into the neighborhood. When he saw how badly the hill was disrupted by its internal hates, he considered the monkeys an easy prey to attack and eat at his leisure. One morning he came close to the hill to plan his campaign, but when the monkeys guessed his purpose, their quarrels were immediately healed. At once they pressed together, their arms intertwined, affirming their loyalty to one another; then, working together in harmony, they rained such a shower of stones on their enemy and rolled such heavy boulders down the side of the hill that the tiger, intimidated by their solidarity, turned and ran into the jungle.

The animals who tried to mediate the quarrels of the monkeys, but without success, said to one another, "Apparently the only thing that will unite the monkey hill is disaster."

42

the dog and her rival

A DOG WHO HAD BEEN
greatly loved by her master found her life less pleasant
after he married. She came one night to talk things over
with the mare and said, "I wish them both happiness.
Perhaps it would be better if I went away, because it
must grieve my master to see the way his wife humiliates
me all day long."

The mare thought that would be a sensible thing to
do, but the dog sighed, shook her head, and continued,
"No, that would never work out, because if I disappeared
without a word, the uncertainty of my fate would break
my master's heart; and, besides, that wife of his would
make him believe I was fickle and had abandoned him,
and he'd never know how much I had suffered or how
great my love was. On second thought, it might be even

simpler if I took poison and died on his doorstep. That I think would be the noblest thing to do, the final proof of my love."

The mare said that such renunciation seemed a generous gesture indeed, and the dog lifted her head and stared at the moon. "I'd do it, too," she said; "I'd kill myself on my master's doorstep if only I could hear his pleas for forgiveness when he finds my body, or see him beating his worthless wife for having driven me to such an end."

Love can be the most dreadful disguise that hate assumes.

43

the identical crows

TWO CROWS HAD AN
argument as to which was the fairer, and the other animals, tiring of the endless debate, suggested that the
woodcutter, known to all as a just man, be called in to
settle the matter. The woodcutter consented, and the two
crows appeared before him. Each in turn exhibited himself, turning out his wings and arching his neck so that it
would be plain to all that he was, as he maintained,
fairer than his competitor; but after the woodcutter had
examined them both, he scratched his head and said:

"So far as I can see, you are exactly alike, and when
things are equally black, there's little profit in drawing
distinctions."

[82]

44

the panther
and the woodcutter

THERE WAS ONCE A PANTHER who, famished by a cold winter, became so bold that he crept up to a woodcutter's cottage and tried to lure the owner outside so that he could eat him. He tapped on the window and stood in the dark while the woodcutter cracked his shutters and asked who had summoned him from his bed. The panther made his voice soft and seductive. He said, "I'm a rich traveler, and I've lost my way in the forest. If you'll come outside and show me the road, I'll reward you with a bagful of gold."

"I'm not interested in gold," said the woodcutter. "What can gold buy that I value?"

The panther said, "Then I promise to take you to my kingdom and give you great power. Everybody will bow down when you pass by."

"That would be tiresome," said the woodcutter. "I can think of nothing sillier than having people bow down when I take a walk." He closed his shutters and got back into bed at once.

Then the defeated panther slunk off to the edge of the forest and lay down, pressing his famished belly against the earth, but his tricks were not all used up, and he began to moan and sob like a man in distress. "Save me! Save me!" he cried. "Save me from the panther who is going to eat me!"

At that the woodcutter ran out of his cottage without calculating the danger, bent only on doing a merciful deed, and a moment later the panther sprang and fixed his teeth in the man's throat, bearing him down to the frozen earth and shaking out the little life that remained in him. When he had finished his meal, the panther rolled his eyes and said, "I've learned an important lesson tonight: some men are betrayed more easily through compassion than through avarice."

45

good news and bad news

A FARMER, HEARING THAT a band of robbers were nearby, sent his wife to the village for safety. Later, when it was reported the robbers had left the neighborhood, he went to the hare and asked him to run at once to the village and tell his wife the good news. "What's the rush about?" asked the hare. "Everything's all right now, isn't it? I'll carry your message tomorrow."

And so things went for a week; then, unexpectedly, the robbers returned. Their first victim was the young farmer, and after they had taken his stores and cattle, they burned his barns and took him away to be sold into slavery. When the hare heard the news, he jumped up and said, "Get out of my way, everybody! I've got to tell the farmer's wife as quick as I can!" He sprang over a nettle patch and ran down the road as fast as he could, since feet are always swift in the service of sorrow.

46

the woodchuck
and the old bones

A WOODCHUCK MADE HIS home in a cemetery, between two ancient graves, and after he had dug his burrow, he came above ground and examined the inscription on the headstone to the right of his doorway. He read:

> "A warrior brave, he did not yield,
> Nor put aside his ashen bow.
> With flashing eye he won each field,
> And conquered every foe."

The woodchuck stared in surprise; then he went below to see which was correct—his own eye or the poet's illusion. When he came back, he turned to the headstone on the left and read:

> "A perfumed lily sent by God,
> She sweetened plain and dell,
> Till jealous Death did seal her up,
> That he alone might smell."

At that the woodchuck lay in the sunlight; but all he could think of to say was, "Well!"

47

the turtle and the geese

A FARMER HAD A NUMBER of geese who ate, swam in the pond, and lived happily despite the fact that their master on market days drove them into pens and chopped off the heads of those he wanted to sell in the village.

One day an old tortoise, who had seen many generations of geese progress from goslings to the chopping block, asked how the geese could be so content with their lot when their eventual fate was so easy to foretell; but the geese hissed scornfully and said: "The chopping block may be the fate of others, but obviously it's a thing that doesn't concern us: if it did, we wouldn't be alive at this moment, now would we?"

Disaster is something that happens to others.

48

the panthers, the leopards, and the jaguars

FOR MANY YEARS THE jaguars had lived at peace with their neighbors, the leopards and the panthers, and then, these latter two having become enemies, the jaguars found themselves caught in between. Now, the jaguars didn't like the governments of either of their neighbors and said so, but to their surprise, they found the doctrines of both had penetrated their own land to such an extent that it was impossible to say in some instances which inhabitant of their country was a jaguar, which a panther, which a leopard.

Since the jaguars wanted to preserve their own customs and government, they decided to examine their suspect citizens individually to determine where their loyalties really were. The first citizen examined said, "I'm a true jaguar, and I love my native country, with its tolerance for all. I despise the leopards and all they stand for, and I'll gladly exterminate them."

The foreman of the committee said, "We know, now, how you feel about leopards; but tell us what you think of panthers. Do you despise panthers, too?" The citizen was silent, shifting about in his chair. "I love my free, native country," he said loudly. "I am a jaguar, the same as yourselves."

The foreman, staring at the protesting patriot, said, "You classified yourself by your reservations, and it's plain you are, in your heart, neither a jaguar nor a leopard, but a panther."

The truth is revealed more often by what one will not say than by what one does.

49

the woodcutter and the lion

A WOODCUTTER AND A LION struck up a friendship. They were forever playing pranks on each other or arguing which was the stronger, a lion or a man. The small animals of the underbrush took pleasure in these disputes, and whenever the lion and the man met, they would hide nearby, chattering together and laughing at the talk.

One day the lion came to where the woodcutter was working and sat down with a show of importance. In his mouth was the thigh bone of an ox, and when he had the woodcutter's attention, he said, "You'll have to admit that a lion's mouth is more powerful than a man's. See, with one movement of my jaw I can crack the thick thigh bone of an ox." The woodcutter spat and leaned against the axe. After a moment he pointed to a nearby boulder and said, "Can you crack that big rock with your mouth, too?"

The animals of the underbrush squealed with pleasure, flicking their tails from side to side and nudging one another in anticipation of the fun. "No," said the lion. "I can't and neither can you."

The woodcutter turned and looked down the road. A party of peasants on their way to the village was approaching, and the woodcutter said, "Do you want to see me do it?"

"Yes," said the lion, confident that he had the better of his friend this time.

At once the woodcutter made excited motions to the peasants. When he had their attention, he cupped his mouth with his hands and shouted, "I've made a discovery: the inside of that rock over there is gold."

Instantly the peasants swarmed over the fields and into the wood, and in a few moments the boulder lay at the lion's feet, cracked not in one place but a dozen. The animals of the underbrush, who are so much easier to amuse than the general reader, hurled themselves about in an ecstasy of mirth and said, "The lion can crack the thick thigh bone of an ox, but a man's mouth is so strong he can crack rocks with it."

50

the hyena and the badger

MEN CAME INTO THE forest one day and began cutting the trees. The animals were alarmed and sent the badger to investigate and make a report. He came back in a day or two and said, "The men are not here to harm us. They are building a sawmill."

The fox, feeling the meeting had been too short, called on the hyena for a few additional words. The hyena explained that actually he had nothing to say, since he had not seen the workmen or the sawmill they were building. He apologized for his lack of precise information, but he promised to do the best he could under the circumstances.

He began to talk rapidly. He recapitulated the history of man and his invention, paying particular attention to the part sawmills had played in his development; he discussed the nature of man, contrasting it with the nature of other animals; he worked out formulas for a better understanding between the two; and at the end of two hours he was still talking, while his audience one by one slipped down from their seats and went home.

Those with nothing to say need many words to say it.

51

the magician and the mole

A MAGICIAN, HIDING FROM
his enemies, took refuge in a cave. While there, he met
a mole who promised to guide him safely through the
tunnels that he and his kind had built, and as they
passed through the passages together, the magician said,
"Why do you live underground where you can neither
see nor appreciate the beauties of the world?"

The mole said, "I am blind, like all my kind; therefore there's no point in living anywhere except in this
dark place."

[96]

The magician offered his sympathy, but the mole said, "It isn't so bad as you think. Sometimes I meet people like yourself from the beautiful upper world, and I listen to the things they tell me, so now, to defeat my blindness, I sit alone in the dark and let my mind fill with wonderful images."

Later, the magician made a spell, and the mole broke upward through the crust of the earth; and sure enough, just as the magician had promised, he saw the world clearly. The magician stood by, waiting his friend's gratitude, but the mole covered his eyes and said, "No! No!—You've played a cruel trick on me. It isn't like this at all!"

52

man and his natural enemy

HIS SUBJECT THAT
morning was a favorite one among Wittin teachers:
Man's superiority to the other animals. His pupils listened and nodded lazily, and then one of them asked,
"How do we know these things are true? What proof
have we got?"

The professor said, "If you'll look about you, you'll see that each animal has some stronger animal that preys upon it, in accordance with those laws of All-seeing Nature which we have just pointed out. Only man has no natural enemy to hunt him down and destroy him. Isn't it self-evident, therefore, that man stands at the top of the ladder of all living things, responsible only to the gods?"

The professor paused, for just then there were loud noises outside the classroom windows. A runaway slave had escaped from his owner, it appeared, and was being pursued by a crowd through the streets. They caught him in the park, not far from some rhododendron bushes, and after they had torn him to pieces, the professor and his pupils went back to their benches. Only the enquiring student remained by the window, and when the professor asked if there were any other questions, he lowered his eyes and said, "No."

53

the traitorous jackal

A JACKAL CAME TO THE
farmers, the enemies of his kind, and said that he had
repudiated his own people and from that day on he
wanted to be thought of as a farmer, not as a jackal; but
being a jackal in reality and familiar with secrets of his
kind, he was of great help to the farmers, and as a result
of his guidance, they were soon able to overthrow the
jackals and very nearly exterminate them.

When they had achieved that result, the farmers began to look at the jackal more thoughtfully, for although he seemed as content with the outcome as they themselves were, the fact remained he was a jackal, after all, and not a farmer, and they were ill at ease with him. Finally they called a meeting to discuss the matter and decided that although they were under obligation to the jackal for his services it was to their interest now to destroy him too, pointing out with some justification that since his nature was what it was, he could not be trusted with their secrets either. They added that a creature who would betray his own kind would hardly hesitate to betray strangers too, if the occasion arose.

54

the tears of the rich

A MULE WHO HAD TOILED faithfully all his life became so decrepit that he was no longer able to do his work. His master, seeing the old animal was of no further use, determined to get rid of him, and one night as the mule rested in the barn, thinking with pleasure of the easy days that lay ahead of him, the master entered and put an end to his dreams. He was not a rich man, as many people thought, he said; in fact, compared with some others, he could be considered poor. Things were hard at the moment, and there was every reason to expect they would get worse.

At that the master broke down and rested his head against the old mule's stall. The decision he had been forced to make was a hard one, he said, and it broke his heart to tell his faithful friend that he could no longer afford to keep him. Then, weeping freely, he led the mule outside and turned him loose on the wasteland.

The old mule looked at the rocky land before him and wondered how it would be possible for him to find food for himself. Winter was coming on rapidly; soon the moor would be covered with snow and swept by bitter winds, and there would be no shelter for him. Knowing these things, the old animal was about to protest the injustice of such an ending for his lifetime of faithful service, but when he saw his master's anguished face, he was himself overcome by emotion, and shook his head in sympathy.

"Poor master," he thought. "I won't burden him with my petty troubles." There's no sight in the world so moving as the rich contemplating their own ruin.

55

dishonored prophets

THE ART OF PROPHECY
was held in such high repute among the Wittins that
they found it necessary to crucify those of their oracles
who did not measure up to the niceties of their calling.
And so it was that prophecy became at once the most
honored and the most impermanent profession in the
kingdom; in fact, the hazards so outweighed the benefits
that it seemed reasonable for the calling to disappear
entirely, and this easily might have happened had it not
been for the career of one old man who had practiced
safely for years and who lived now in splendor, honored
by all.

One day this well-loved figure was visited by an
apprentice prophet who wanted to learn from him that
basic wisdom which pleased people and rulers alike, and
after he had made his request, the old prophet said,
"Listen and learn for yourself." He drew back the cur-

tains of his temple and stood before the people who had waited all day for his appearance.

"We plan a war against the Bretts," said an old general. "Tell us if such a war is wise and just."

"It is wise and just to destroy all inferior people, in order that true beauty, culture, and moral worth may survive, and the Wittins have no equals in the world," said the old prophet in a deep voice.

"The farmers want to plant corn," said an official. "Prophesy if the weather will be auspicious or if frost will kill the crops."

"The gods so love the Wittins," said the old prophet, "that they never send bad weather to plague them, as they do to others. If the weather is bad and the young crops blighted, it is only because of forces beyond the control of the gods."

Then the king himself spoke: "They propose a marriage for me with a foreign princess. Is she worthy to be my wife?"

"There's no mortal woman worthy to be the wife of our great king," said the prophet; "but since it is forbidden him to marry a goddess, it's better to take this foreign princess than to go childless. It may be in time that she will take on part of our king's great goodness, and she may acquire under his guidance some of the virtues he possesses, for there is no man so wise, so handsome, so noble as the King of the Wittins."

Having granted his audiences, the old prophet drew

the curtains and turned to the novice. He raised his hand for silence, anticipating the criticism of his disciple, and remarked with a great deal of earned satisfaction, "A prophet with honor is one who repeats the things that others already believe."

56

the wolves
and the work animals

A FARMER, HEARING THAT wolves were heading in the direction of his farm, called his work animals together to organize a defense. The animals listened to their master's words, and the farmer, noticing their submissive bearing and sensing their lack of interest in resisting the wolves, raised his voice reproachfully.

"What has happened to your pride and your instinct to fight for your lives?" he asked. "What has become of your spirit, your self-reliance, your courage?"

At that, the work animals lifted their heads meekly. "Can it be possible you ask us that, Master?" they said.

57

the fat woman and
the terrier

A TERRIER WAS OFTEN taken for a walk by his mistress, a large woman, and as they went down the street, with the terrier tugging at his leash and the fat woman panting a few steps behind, the dog got the idea that he was pulling his mistress along. Sometimes she would stop and talk with a friend, and the terrier, thinking she had broken down on the sidewalk, would pull with such force that his leash was as taut as a violin string. "I declare," said the woman laughing a little, "I never saw such a dog for pulling a body along."

One day as the terrier lay on the window ledge, some other dogs came up. They wanted him to play with them in the street, but he refused. "I'd like to, but I can't," he said. "I've got to take her walking in a few minutes."

"She doesn't need you when she goes walking," said the other dogs. "Where did you get such an idea?"

The terrier said, "Oh, yes she does need me! She gets stuck, and there's nobody who can pull her along like I can."

The other dogs said, "Slip out of your collar the next time you two go walking, and you'll see that your mistress can get along better without you than with you." The terrier did what the others suggested, and to his surprise he saw that they were right. Afterwards he wouldn't go out at all, but lay all day with his nose between his paws. "Why did they show me how unimportant I am?" he asked. "Why did they destroy my one reason for living?"

58

the murderer and his moral code

A MAN CAME TO THE courthouse saying he wanted to give himself up. He had killed his wife and her sweetheart, but he felt no remorse for his deed, and he was convinced no decent-minded jury would convict him. The facts, he explained, were simple, and they were these:

Some months before, he had made arrangements to share his marriage bed with a neighbor, and as a reward the neighbor agreed to pay him a fixed sum of money each month. For a while the neighbor and his wife acted honestly and aboveboard, but lately they planned to elope to another country, thus breaking the contract and depriving him of money that was rightfully his. The face of the prisoner got red with anger at this point, and he said, "So when I found out how low-down they were, how dishonorably they were behaving, I killed them both."

"When did this happen?" asked the judge.

"Late Saturday night."

"Why didn't you give yourself up on Sunday morning instead of waiting a day?"

"What!" the murderer said in a shocked voice. "Report a crime on the Sabbath, God's day of rest?"

The judge turned to his clerk and said, "If there's anything more inconsistent than man's moral code, it hasn't been brought to my attention yet."

59

the king
and the bright young men

EACH SPRING THE KING of the Bretts examined a score of the country's brightest young men, fitting them into that profession or branch of public life where their peculiar talents could be used to the best advantage. One year, to vary the monotony of question and answer, he thought of another way to achieve his end, and when the first candidate came into the room, he said, "A man is traveling down a road. He is stopped by a giant who is sitting on a stone. What happened afterwards?"

The first candidate said: "The traveler, knowing the giant meant to kill him, worked out a plan of defense. He walked up to the giant boldly and kicked him; then he ran in ever narrowing circles, while the giant pursued him. In this way the giant approached the stone unawares, being intent on his capture, stumbled over it, and sprawled on his face. Then, while he was helpless on the ground, the traveler picked up the stone and killed him with it."

"You belong in the army," said the king. "The army, of course."

The next candidate came in, and when given the story he smiled and said: "The giant told the traveler he had a bottle of wine, and had been sitting on the stone waiting for a merry companion to share it with. Then it turned out the traveler had cheese and bread in his sack, which he spread out on the stone, and when the giant and the traveler had eaten and drunk their fill, they sang such jolly songs and were so happy and gay that the whole countryside echoed with their laughter."

The king looked quizzically at this powerful, simple young man. "But wasn't the traveler afraid of the giant?" he asked.

"No," said the candidate. "Why should he be afraid? You see, the traveler was as strong as the giant, or stronger, and knew it from the beginning." The king touched the hand of this young man. "Would you like to be the bodyguard who goes with me everywhere?" he asked; and when the young man laughed and nodded, it was arranged that way.

The third candidate said: "The giant was sitting on the stone because he'd stuck a thorn in his toe and couldn't walk farther; so the traveler removed the thorn and bound up the wound with a bandage he happened to have in his pocket at the time."

The king said, "You're almost too easy. Report to the royal hospital for training."

The fourth man was more complex. He said: "When the traveler knew the giant meant to rob him, he said that he was on a mission for his king and he'd been told to fetch a bag of jewels which were hidden in the woods nearby. The giant was taken in by the story, and thinking to exploit the man's stupidity, he said he'd accompany the traveler to the place where the jewels were hidden to see that no harm came to him on the way. The traveler thanked the giant for this courtesy, and they started inland, but as they walked, the traveler pulled up reeds and plaited them into a strong rope; then when they reached the side of a hill, the traveler said the jewels were hidden beneath the ledge on which they were standing, and as the giant lay flat and stretched his arms downward to reach them, the traveler tied him up with the rope he had made and left him there, after taking for himself the fine gold chain the giant was wearing."

"The diplomatic corps," said the king.

And so things went until the last man was called. When he had heard the situation, he shook his head sadly, and said: "This story can have but one true ending, and it's this: the giant seized the poor helpless traveler and carried him off to his den in the mountains.

There he tossed him into a pit where the other unfortunates he had captured awaited their doom."

At this moment the candidate was overcome with such strong emotion that he could not continue. He beat his breast and cried bitterly. "I can't bear this," he said in a suffering voice. "The traveler's end is too terrible to think about!"

The king rang at that moment and his guards came in. "Have this man's head cut off," he said, and continued in explanation when the captain murmured at his harsh and uncharacteristic conduct, "I can understand a cruel man, and find a place for him; I can understand a compassionate man, and find a place for him as well; but when one man inflicts cruelty and weeps for his victims in the same breath, he is a monster, and if we let him live he will someday destroy us all."

60

the king and the outcast

THE KING OF THE WITTINS, driving through the park with his nobles, came upon a crowd near one of the lakes. When he asked the cause of their assembly, a woman who stood apart from the others said, "My husband drowned himself, and his body has now washed ashore."

"Why should anybody drown himself when life is so splendid?" asked the king.

The woman showed the identifying marks on her wrists, and said, "We are outcasts, as you see. Nobody is allowed to touch us or even to speak to us in a friendly way. We stand aside when others pass us in the road, and we must not complain when they spit on us."

The king was silent, and the woman went on: "Life is hard for all, but for us it was unbearable. We had no food much of the time; we were alone; we had nothing to look forward to but degradation and pain. My husband could no longer endure this existence, and he killed himself, as you see."

The king turned to his nobles. "Do people spit on you in the streets? Do they drive you away with curses when you come too close?"

"No, Your Majesty. That never happens."

The king spoke to his handsome coachmen: "Do you stand aside while others pass you on the road? Do you find life insecure?"

"No, Your Majesty," said the coachmen.

The king turned to the woman and said, "You've heard my questions and their answers. Isn't it plain now that you and your husband only imagined these things?"

The woman covered her head and walked away, not answering the king, knowing that understanding comes from experience, and from experience alone.

61

the end of the world

AT ONE POINT IN THEIR history, the Bretts were attacked and conquered by their neighbors. One man who escaped the general slaughter took refuge in an old field deep in the forest, and when he realized that he was safe, he threw himself on the ground and wept. After a time the field animals came to investigate, and when he saw them, he said, "How can you be so unconcerned? Don't you know the world was destroyed this morning?"

The animals looked at one another in surprise. "Was the world really destroyed this morning?" they asked.

"Only I escaped," said the weeping man. "I am the last Brett."

"Are you sure the world was destroyed?" asked the animals, and added, "Excuse us for doubting your word, but in this field alone there are, at this moment, millions of creatures alive and breathing and leading their natural lives."

62

the snapping turtle and the wisteria vine

OF ALL THE CREATURES of the forest, the snapping turtle was the most tenacious: once he seized an enemy in his jaws, he wouldn't turn loose until his adversary admitted he was beaten or until it thundered. One day he was crawling through the underbrush when a big snake, hanging down from a tree, swung forward and struck him between his near-sighted eyes. The turtle stopped in his tracks, wondering if the affront were intentional or not; then deciding it was not, he continued on his way, saying over his shoulder, "Do that again and I'll bite you; and if I bite you, I'll hold on until you admit you've had enough or until it thunders. I have great strength of character, as anybody will tell you, and I mean what I say."

He'd hardly finished before the snake swung back, this time catching the turtle in the rear. The turtle, furious at the insult, seized the tail of the snake in his jaws—and instantly he knew his poor eyesight had betrayed him again. It wasn't a snake at all; it was only the dangling end of an old wisteria vine.

For a time the turtle hung on, knowing he had made a mistake but unwilling to act contrary to the traditions of his kind, and after a while the other animals gathered to watch the spectacle of a live turtle fighting a dead wisteria vine. "It's nothing but a vine," they said. "The vine can't admit it's beaten, so why don't you turn loose and go home to supper?"

"I'll turn loose when it thunders, and not before," said the turtle. He glanced upward, but there was not a cloud in the sky, and it looked as though it would stay fair for a long time. And so things went, with the friends of the turtle urging him to turn loose and with him shaking his head stubbornly. "When it thunders," he said. "Not until it thunders."

Nobody was surprised when, toward the end of the week, the turtle died and fell to the ground. His friends gathered about him and said, "Sometimes it's hard to tell the difference between strength of character and plain stupidity."

63

the screech owl
and the farmer

A SCREECH OWL JUST learning to talk flew into a tree to practice the one word he knew, a word his mother had taught him that morning. He seated himself on a limb and arranged his feathers to his satisfaction, but before he had a chance to speak, a farmer ploughing in the fields below him pulled up his team, took off his hat, and scratched his head uncertainly. "I declare," said the farmer to himself. "I believe I made a mistake in planting corn this year. My brother-in-law told me to put in oats instead."

"Who?" asked the screech owl in a small, quavering voice.

The farmer turned around, but not seeing anybody, he came to the conclusion that some stranger was sitting in the tree to his left, hidden by the foliage. "My brother-in-law told me," he repeated politely. "He's the one I'm talking about. He's a tall, sandy-haired man with a red face."

"Who? Who? Who?" asked the little owl in his base register, and this time he managed to put contempt into the falling inflection of the word. "Who?" he said again, and then, as if running up and down the scale, he repeated, "Who-o-o? Who-o-o?" as though he were laughing at the farmer, his brother-in-law, and their pretensions.

The farmer left his team and came to the fence. He broke a club from a dead apple tree and said angrily, "If somebody I know doesn't act more civil in the future, that somebody is going to get his head knocked off." He waited, swinging his stick, and then the young screech owl, getting more and more sure of himself, lifted his neck and shouted in the shrillest, most penetrating voice. "Wh-o-o-o? Wh-o-o-o?"

"*You,* that's who!" said the enraged farmer. He hurled his club into the tree in the direction of the voice, and the surprised little owl was knocked off his perch; then, when he saw the farmer breaking another limb from the apple tree, he gathered himself together and flew back to his mother as fast as he could manage it, having learned, without the loss of too many feathers, the fate of those who ask questions for the pleasure of hearing their own voices.

[123]

64

the queen
and the woodcutter's wife

SHE HAD FINISHED WASH-
ing her pots when she looked up and saw a royal party
approaching; then a page boy sounded a call on a
trumpet, and she came to her door wiping her hands on
her apron. The captain of the party said that the Queen
of the Wittins had become faint while driving through
the woods, and on being told that a woodcutter's hut was
nearby, had decided to rest there until she recovered.

The woodcutter's wife moved about her house dusting her chairs and benches and smoothing two wrinkles out of her bed, and when the queen entered, magnificent in satin and lace, and hung from head to foot with jewels, everything was as decent as the poor wife could make it; but the queen wouldn't lie down as the poor wife suggested, nor would she take off her cloak nor loosen her corset.

The woodcutter's wife went to her window and looked out. She saw that the horsemen had placed themselves about the hut in a circle and sat at attention with their swords drawn. At the front and back doors of the hovel, a special sentry stood and looked in, watching every move the queen made. "You could loosen your corset and take your shoes off too if those men weren't looking at you," said the woodcutter's wife in a whisper. "Why don't you send them away and make yourself comfortable?"

Then the queen, amused at the woman's simplicity, explained that while an ordinary woman could do such a thing, it was beneath the dignity of a great queen.

The woodcutter's wife went to her cupboard and poured out a glass of milk. "At least you can refresh yourself with cool milk," she said. "Folks hereabouts say I've got the best cow in the neighborhood." But as she approached the queen, the sentries sprang forward and spilled the milk on the floor.

The queen, seeing how puzzled the woodcutter's wife was and pitying her stupidity, explained the situation.

"I'm not allowed to eat or drink anything which hasn't been prepared specially for me," she said. She lifted her head proudly and continued, "Poisoners, you know! All great people have enemies who would like to destroy them."

When the queen had recovered from her faintness, she went to her carriage, and the procession prepared to move away, while the woodcutter's wife stood on her doorstep watching; then, thinking of her queen, she began to cry, wiping her eyes on her petticoat. "Poor little thing," she said. "I don't see how she stands it. Thank God for giving me a happy, carefree life!"

The queen turned in her carriage and looked at the weeping woodcutter's wife. She was touched by the sight, and turning to her captain she said, "I'm afraid we've done the good woman a disservice. Before we came, she was content to live as she does, not knowing any better, but now we've given her a glimpse of paradise and then shut the door in her face."

Those we pity most would often be surprised if they knew.

65

the king and the plotters

AT ONE TIME IN THEIR
history the Bretts had a merciful and just king, and
during his reign there were few offenses for which he
could not find an excuse, and pardon. Things went well
for a time, and then a plot to kill the good monarch
came to light. The king asked to interview the plotters,
in order to find out their grievances against him, and so
the ringleaders were called, and soon stood before him.

"Do you have a personal reason for hating me?" he asked. "Do I oppress you in any way?"

"No," said the prisoners.

"Do you know another country where people have as much freedom and happiness as they have here?"

"No," said the prisoners.

"Then tell me why you want to kill me?" asked the king.

After a pause, one of the prisoners spoke up: "Everybody knows how good you are, and so we figured it this way: if we killed you, and the plot succeeded, we'd be safe, being on the winning side; if we failed, we still had nothing to fear, because we knew you'd let us go free afterwards."

The king turned to his guards and said, "Take these men back and see that the sentence of the court is carried out, because a man who permits himself to be destroyed by his own virtues is not merciful, but a fool."

66

the sow
with the unlimited milk

THERE WAS ONCE A FARMER
with a spotted sow, the pride of his life. He boasted of
her at the inn, saying she not only gave birth to big
litters at quick intervals, but protected her young with
devotion and had an unlimited supply of milk for their
stomachs as well.

One day a delegation came to see if the farmer's claims
were true. They leaned above the sty and watched the
sow with her newest brood, and at last they admitted the
farmer's boasts seemed justified, although they still
doubted the sow's milk was unlimited, as he maintained.
In their opinion, she merely had enough milk, and no
more, to feed her shoats with, the same as less fertile
sows. Listening to the talk, the sow had a new feeling of

importance, and she determined to confirm her master's wildest boasts when next an opportunity arose.

This occasion came a day or two later, when the master was called away, and hardly had he disappeared down the road before she spoke to her sister on the right. What the master had said publicly about her was true, she explained: the supply of her milk was really unlimited, and she would accept as her own the four pigs her neighbor was trying to raise. The next day she took five additional pigs from the red sow back of the barn, and before the week had passed, every sow on the farm had given up her pigs to the sow with unlimited milk.

Her own litter, shoved aside by their foster brothers and sisters, cried piteously, saying they had got only a drop of milk the whole day; but their mother answered them fairly, as she had answered the pigs who were not her own: "Then fill your stomachs with water, for my milk is so powerful that one drop is all you need."

When the farmer returned, he came to the pen of his beloved sow, but the sight he saw made him turn away with grief, for there before his eyes lay all the young pigs of his farm, dead of starvation. The spotted sow waited his praise, lifting her eyes to his own, but the farmer cursed her instead for bringing about his ruin, just as her young had cursed her before they died. "Alas!" said the spotted sow. "I've learned, now that it's too late, that no sow, however talented, can feed more than her own litter."

67

the cock and the capon

A COCK IN CHARGE OF a barnyard of hens lifted his neck, crowed, and said to his friend, the capon: "Why do you complain that because of the injustice done you, you never know love? Love is a monotonous matter of little importance. Be glad you're not mixed up in it."

One morning the farmer penned up the cock with a flock of geese, who didn't interest him in the least, and the capon came to visit him after a time; but the cock had changed his tune a little, and sticking his neck through a knothole in the fence, he said, "I want to amend what I said and restate the matter this way: Love is of little importance so long as you can have the particular thing you want."

68

the hangman and the hero

THE WITTINS REGARDED
the taking of life with such repugnance that they required their hangman to wear a costume which made his profession known to all. He must live in a house beyond the limits of the city; he could walk certain streets, but only at designated hours; and he must ring a bell as he went along, so that others would not be contaminated by some accidental contact.

As he was returning home on one occasion, the hangman got a stone in his shoe, and without thinking sat down under the marble statue that the people had erected to their hero-god, the fierce warrior who had founded their nation. For a time the hangman was so occupied that he did not notice a crowd had gathered, but when they threw stones at him and shouted that he had corrupted this, their most sacred spot, by sitting upon it, the hangman ran for his life; and although the mob was close behind him at times, he managed to escape them at last.

An old tortoise, who had witnessed the chase, asked what had happened, and the hangman told him. "But I don't blame the Wittins," he said. "I brought it on myself."

"What did you do that was wrong?"

The hangman, from long habit, picked up his bell and tinkled it to the rhythm of his words. "I'm a hangman, as you see. I take the lives of people, so when I sat on a step of the monument, I defiled the memory of our great hero."

The old tortoise thought this over and then said, "But the hero whose monument you sat on took the lives of people, too. Now, tell me why one of you should be reviled and the other revered for doing the same thing."

The hangman stared at the tortoise, marveling at his stupidity. "Tortoises haven't intelligence enough to understand these distinctions," he said. "So don't discuss matters you know nothing about."

"Perhaps you're right," said the old tortoise. "Perhaps if our brains could accept contradictions without conflict, we wouldn't have remained tortoises for a million years, as we have, but would have developed into something as powerful as man, who rules the universe."

69

the doubting ducks

A FOX HAD HIS EYES on a flock of ducks, but at his approach they would back away from him, ready to take flight if he came nearer. "What have I done? Why do you mistrust me so?" he asked in a hurt voice.

"It's because you're so strange," they said, "so different from ourselves."

The next day when the ducks came to the pond, they saw the fox quacking and swimming about. "What are you doing on the shore when the water is so fine today?" he called out loudly.

The ducks, still a little suspicious, watched the fox at his antics, but when he upended himself as well as the best of them, dived down among the reeds, and caught a frog, their last doubts vanished. "The fox is like ourselves," they said. "There's no danger in him at all."

70

the pig and the dirty doves

A PIG, WHOSE PEN WAS built against a barn, noticed that the farmer had put up a dovecote near his sty. When he realized the affront, the pig trembled with rage, protesting to the other animals. He said, "I don't understand why the farmer put those dirty doves where I must look at them all day! He wouldn't have done it, either, if I hadn't been buried in mud up to my snout at the time and couldn't see what was going on."

"Are doves especially dirty?" asked the cow.

"Dirty!" said the enraged pig. "Look for yourself and see how they foul their own nests and wallow in the filth they've made. It's enough to make anybody sick!"

The cow wrinkled her brow but remained silent.

"The sight of the doves living in filth is bad enough," continued the pig, "but as if that weren't enough, they must roll on the roof all day and make a silly grunting noise in their throats."

The pig flounced off, grunting angrily, while the cow shook her head, thinking how objectionable we find our own faults when we see them manifested in others.

71

the mink
and the tame animals

A MINK WHO HAD
traveled and seen much of the world made friends with a
group of barnyard animals, and when their work for the
day was done, he would creep up to the edge of the yard
and talk with them. The experiences of the barnyard
animals were as limited as those of the mink were varied,
so they found him, with his stories of travel and adventure, a pleasant companion indeed. One day he men-
tioned a flock of wild sheep with whom he had spent a
winter, and the sheep of the barnyard looked at him
with disbelief. "Sheep aren't wild," they said. "Sheep
live only where there are men who need their wool and
their flesh."

The mink said, "There are many wild sheep. In fact, before mankind made them work for him, all animals were wild and lived as they pleased, completely happy and free."

"Were cattle free, too?" asked the ox.

"Yes, of course," said the mink. "So were geese, hens, horses, goats, and every other creature."

The animals were excited and asked questions, and the mink pointed out to them the differences between a life of freedom and a life of bondage to show how much they had lost, how unfortunate their lot was, as compared with their untamed brothers'.

When he had finished, the animals, who had previously taken their servitude for granted, pressed closely about him and said, "What's to be done now? How can we get our freedom back?"

"I don't know," said the mink. "Perhaps nothing can be done about it now."

At this the barnyard animals wept and swayed their heads from side to side. "Then why did you tell us?" they asked. "Why did you show us how miserable we are, if nothing can be done to help us?"

72

the philosophical lead-ram

THERE WAS ONCE A LEAD-
ram who lived in a slaughterhouse and whose duty was
to guide his kind to their deaths. The sheep never
questioned his authority, and once he had organized
them into columns for the convenience of their execu-
tioners, they would trot obediently behind him with
downcast heads; and they were so docile, so meek, that
they did not notice when he slipped out of line at the
right moment and left them tricked and carried to their
deaths by the weight of their own forward-pressing
bodies.

Later, from a place of safety beside the runway, the lead-ram would watch his brothers calmly, for in his security he had became a philosopher, and when his victims, seeing the sharp knives that waited them, rolled their eyes, bleated, and struggled to escape, he would point out to them that sheep were born to be slaughtered and that they should feel only pride in the fulfillment of their destinies. Death was a trivial thing at best, he maintained. Ideas were the things that really counted.

And so it went until one day the lead-ram forgot to step aside at the right instant and, to his dismay, found himself caught on the belts along with his brothers. At first he was quiet, fortified with philosophy, but when he saw the knives coming closer, he too began to struggle and bleat in terror, just as his victims did, knowing at last that those who send others to their deaths with fortitude are usually sure that they themselves are safe.

73

the guinea fowl and the farmer

A GUINEA FOWL LIVED in a wasteland near the melon patch of a farmer. At night when the farmer and his wife were asleep, the guinea fowl would fly to the patch and pick out the melon he wanted to eat; then he would peck a hole big enough for his neck, insert his clown-like head, and eat the meat inside. The farmer's wife, noticing each morning that a melon had been destroyed, urged her husband to set a trap for the thief, but he only smiled and said, "What he takes will never be missed. Let him have his melon now and then."

[142]

When the guinea fowl saw he was not molested, he grew more and more arrogant. "What kind of man is this?" he asked himself. "He hasn't even got courage enough to defend his own property." In his insolence he began destroying the young melons before they ripened on the vines and pecking holes in the ripe ones that he did not want for himself. "The farmer won't do anything about it," he said. "The farmer is afraid of me."

The farmer, aroused by the senseless destruction of his crop, loaded his gun and lay that night behind a blind he had made, and when the guinea fowl flew up from the wasteland, he fired both barrels, and the fowl fell dead before him. "Your fate," he said to the dead bird, "is the fate of those who mistake tolerance for weakness."

74

the doctor
and the hippopotamus

A YOUNG ORANGUTAN WAS ambitious to cure the ills of others, and when he saw how often his friends died because a bone or some other object was lodged in their throats, he decided to specialize in that branch of healing. Gradually stories of his skill were told all over the jungle, and when the hippopotamus yawned one morning and got a log crosswise in his gullet, he sent for the orangutan as a matter of course.

[144]

The doctor came promptly, but although he tried all his instruments and even stretched his arm forward as far as it would reach, he couldn't touch the log, much less remove it. As a last resort, he asked the hippopotamus to raise his neck and stretch his jaws even wider, and when he did so, the doctor walked into his mouth, braced himself, and tugged with all his might at the obstruction.

The log came away unexpectedly, and at the same instant the hippopotamus flinched and swallowed. Then, when he had got his breath again, he began smelling about for his benefactor, not realizing he had swallowed his doctor when he swallowed the log, nor knowing that it is the fate of specialists to perish of their own specialties.

75

cowards and fearless men

A CHIPMUNK AND A RABBIT, concluding that their natural timidity was their best protection against the dangerous world about them, formed a partnership which they found advantageous. When they were looking for food, one of them would remain on guard while the other searched, and at the first unfamiliar scent from the brush, the first unexpected movement in the grass, he would call out to his companion and they would scamper to cover, lying there with wildly beating hearts until their world was a safe place to move about in once more.

One day a lion, who took a lordly interest in their welfare, said, "When you hunt in the future, come with me and feel no anxiety whatever, because I fear nothing that lives, and I'm strong enough to protect you from your enemies." After that, the two animals hunted boldly with the lion until one day the three of them met a man with a gun. The chipmunk and the rabbit halted, trembled, and began backing away, but the fearless lion upbraided them. "Well, what are you afraid of this time?" he asked humorously. "Haven't you got me to protect you?" Then he roared and sprang into the clearing, but before he had a chance to strike down the hunter, the latter raised his rifle and fired, and the lion fell dead at his feet.

The chipmunk and the rabbit did not wait to see more. They turned and ran desperately, while the bullets from the hunter's gun whistled about their ears. When they were safe again, the chipmunk said, "We were fools to hunt with the lion, because it's obvious now that there's no companion more dangerous than one without fear."

76

the visitor
and the razorback hogs

ONE DAY AS A FORESTER and his friend from the city were walking in the woods, a peculiar, stropping sound came to their ears. The noise got more pronounced as they went along, and at last the visitor saw its source: before him, at the edge of a glade, a hundred half-starved pigs were rubbing their backs against trees. The visitor started back at the sight, but the forester said, "There's nothing to be afraid of. It's only a herd of razorback hogs stropping themselves."

The forester threw a pine cone at the pigs, and at once they squealed and ran away. "You see?" he said. "Razorbacks won't hurt anybody."

"Then why are they always sharpening themselves?" asked the visitor.

The forester said, "I don't know. I suppose it's just their nature to strop themselves."

The visitor turned back to the village. "Maybe I'm too easily alarmed," he said, "but it seems to me that creatures who spend so much time sharpening their weapons will some day find occasion to use them."

77

the lark and her nest

TWO MEN WERE WALKING through a barley field when a lark sprang up and circled above their heads. At first the men paid no attention to her, but when she didn't fly away, as was to be expected, they stopped and watched her behavior. After a while, the lark lighted in the field again and made a chirping sound, running down the row ahead of them, spreading her wings, and glancing over her shoulder.

"How strangely the lark is behaving," said one of the men. "She acts as if she were trying to coax us away from this spot." The other man, more experienced in such matters, said, "Her nest is nearby, and she's afraid we'll find it."

At that the two men began bending back the barley, and after a short search they found the lark's nest and divided her eggs between them.

Nothing betrays us so quickly as our little efforts to deceive.

78

the birthday of the hermit

A HERMIT HAD SO ENDEARED himself to the defenseless animals of the forest and field that they wanted to bring him presents on his birthday as a sign of their affection. The day when it came was mild and sunny, and the creatures he had protected so well gathered at the appointed place and chattered gaily.

Since the hermit had loved birds more than all other living things, it was fitting that the present the birds made for him should be the finest of all. It was a blanket of the softest and most beautiful down imaginable. The migratory birds had gathered the material from every part of the earth; then the weaving birds had taken it and had woven it into gaily colored patterns.

The birds with their soft and brilliant blanket flew at

the head of the column, moving their wings slowly and singing the song they had composed in honor of the hermit, a song which told in detail of the merciful things he had done for their kind; after them came the squirrels, the hares, the fawns, and the other small animals, each bearing his individual gift of flowers, fruits, or honey.

And so the procession moved happily until they reached the side of the mountain and saw the hermit's cave in front of them. At that instant the animals became quiet, listened, and looked at one another; and in the silence they heard plainly the groans and cries of pain that came from inside the cave. They sped anxiously to the cave's opening and peered in, and what they saw made them drop their gifts and start back in dismay, for the hermit with his feet and hands caught in vises lay twisting on a mattress of thorns.

The animals, thinking their friend had been thus treated by some barbarous enemy, ran forward to release him, but the hermit stopped them, saying that since this was his birthday, he was reminded anew of his sins and was undergoing this pain as an atonement for them; then, moving his head from side to side, he cried out, "Leave me to my suffering! I am not worthy of your sympathy! I am completely vile!"

The birds and the small animals, seeing they could do nothing, turned sadly and went away, wondering how one so merciful to others could be so merciless to himself.

79

men and the other animals

A TRAVELER PITCHED HIS
tent for the night, and the animals of the forest, who had
never before seen a man, sat near his fire, asking him
questions about the customs of his country and the habits
of his kind.

The traveler told in detail of men and the civilization
they had built; then, seeing the puzzled expressions on
the faces of his audience, he added, "Man and animals

like yourselves are so different that it's hard for you to take in what I'm saying. Now, don't be offended, but animals like you, as everybody knows, are cruel, treacherous, and inclined to be thieving, while man, on the other hand, is of divine origin and has a soul. Man is gentle, kind, and noble, and, unlike other animals, his life is regulated, not by chance, but by a moral code. For instance, to give you some idea of what a man's moral nature is, let me tell you that in my country alone there are ten thousand laws for the suppression of every possible offense."

There was silence, and then one of the animals spoke in a bewildered voice: "If men are noble and generous and compassionate, as you say, why do they find it necessary to protect themselves against one another's goodness so carefully?"

80

the disasters

A WOMAN WHO LIVED alone with her mother returned home one day to find her street in a state of commotion. People strode up and down on the cobblestones, shouting and making gestures, and in front of her particular gate a crowd had gathered, talking rapidly, waving their arms about, and clutching their heads in their hands. The woman, alarmed by this time, hurried forward and asked the reason for the excitement.

One of the neighbors said, "The Wittins have declared war on us and are now crossing our borders, destroying everything in their path."

At that, the woman sat on her doorstep, cried with relief, and said, "Oh, thank Heaven! For a minute I thought Mama had fallen and hurt her hip again."

81

the untouchable

A TRAVELER, HAVING LOST his way in the mountains, took refuge for the night in a cave; but he saw at once that another had preceded him and was now warming himself before a fire of sticks and leaves. When the traveler entered, the other man said, "I'm an untouchable. Be careful not to stumble and fall against me."

The traveler sat on the other side of the fire, watching his companion and wondering what factor made one of them an honorable man and the other an outcast. Not finding any great physical difference between them, he thought perhaps the solution lay in another field, and he said, "Tell me, do you feel hate and joy and love, as I do? Are you capable of feeling hope and jealousy and regret?"

"Yes," said the untouchable. "I feel all those things. I also feel shame, envy, sorrow, and pity."

And so the two men talked, trying to discover some difference between them but not succeeding; then the traveler said, "As far as I can see, we are very much alike"; and added, "do you know why you're an untouchable and I am not?"

"No," said the other, "I only know I was born an untouchable of parents who were like myself."

There was a long silence, while the two men examined each other across the fire, and then the traveler said, "I wonder what would happen if I touched you?"

"I don't know," said the other. "Nobody has done it so far."

The eyes of the traveler widened at his own audacity, and he said, "You know?—I'm going to touch you and find out." The outcast drew back against the wall and covered his eyes, but the traveler stretched out his arms and touched the untouchable. After a time the outcast asked in a frightened voice, "Did the mountain totter? Did the rivers dry up? Did the moon fall out of the sky?"

The traveler said in astonishment, "Nothing at all happened. Everything's precisely as it was before."

82

the nightingale that
listened to men

A NIGHTINGALE, SO LACK-
ing in fear that he built his nest in a tree beside the palace
of the King of the Wittins, listened to the court poet as
he recited the poem he had composed that day, marking
how often the poet spoke of nightingales and their song;
for the poet and the people who heard his verses sighed
when they remembered how short a season the nightingales spent in their kingdom and how even during that
brief time the birds hid themselves in forests so remote
that the song was wasted on woodmen and charcoal-
burners.

Hearing these things, the nightingale determined to

give the Wittins the pleasure they wanted, and so he flew to the forest and told his kind what the poet had said. At once they hit on the idea of serenading their patrons from the wooded park in the center of the city, and that night they assembled in the grove and distributed themselves among the trees; then, upon a prearranged signal, they lifted their heads and sang with notes of such soft concentrated ardor that their feathers puffed out and trembled with the vibration of their throats.

The Wittins, hearing the music, came to their windows and listened, speaking to one another loudly, calling attention to the angelic nature of the serenade, and commenting on their individual reactions to an event which was, at once, so unforeseen and so beautiful; but as the music swelled in volume, the people were forced to talk louder and louder in order to make themselves understood, until at length their voices were drowned out by music so heavenly that nothing like it had ever been heard in the world before; and when the Wittins could no longer hear themselves, they became frightened. Their faces got red with anger, and they began to shout and make threatening gestures; but the nightingales mistaking these things for applause, continued the slow rise and fall of their song. In panic the Wittins rushed out of their houses, seized stones and sticks and hurled them furiously at the trees.

Later the nightingales who had survived the fury of the Wittins held a council and counted their losses. They demanded that the bird who had persuaded them to undertake the adventure be summoned to explain his actions. They called his name over and over, but there was no answer, for the nightingale who had listened to men and had accepted as truth those valuations with which they beguile themselves, lay at that moment on the ground, his wings broken by a stone, thinking over and over, "No matter what their poets say, the Wittins value but one sound, and that is the harshness of their own voices."

83

the miracle

THE PEOPLE OF A FARAWAY island worshipped the god of the volcano that lifted itself above them. Each day they took him offerings and left them at a shrine near the crater's edge, a shrine their ancestors had built for their most sacred relic: an image of their god which he had made for them with his own hands and had given them to keep as a sign of his favor. For years the volcano had been quiet, and then without warning it threw out clouds of steam and smoke while a rumbling noise came up from its depths. At once the natives got their belongings together and prepared to go to the mainland, wondering in what way they had offended their god.

On this particular day, as it happened, there was a stranger on the island, a merchant who had come to trade, and when he saw the natives departing, he said, "Are you going to abandon your idol to destruction? After all, you can't value your god as highly as you say if none of you is willing to rescue his image from the shrine."

He learned, then, something he'd not been told before: according to the legends of the islanders, the volcano god, when he gave the image of himself to them, had said that as long as they were his children, and his chosen ones, the image would not be destroyed; but if he turned against them beyond hope of forgiveness, he would burn the idol in his own fire. The destruction of the idol was, then, a thing over which they had no control.

Since the merchant was an enlightened man, he didn't believe these foolish things, and he said, "The idol is made of wood, and if you leave it where it is, the lava will burn it up, along with everything else in its path."

The natives moved toward their canoes, carrying their poor possessions. "No," they said. "That cannot happen, unless our god wills it so."

The merchant stood watching them, amazed at the childlike simplicity of their faith. A feeling of pity came over him, and he understood deeply at that instant how hard and barren their lives had been. And when the relic that set them apart was destroyed, they would be lost indeed, for they would not even have hope to sustain them. It was then the merchant risked his life and ran up the side of the volcano, jumping from rock to rock to avoid the rivulets of lava. When he reached the shrine, it was already in flames, but the image was still unharmed, and he took it from its stone altar and hid it under his coat.

Days later, when the volcano was quiet again and the people came back to the island, they went first to the shrine at the edge of the crater; but the merchant had preceded them by a good ten minutes, although they were never to know that, and when the islanders arrived, they saw that a miracle had taken place, for although the burning lava had destroyed everything else, the image rested undamaged on its altar. Instantly they began to pray and sing hymns of thanksgiving; then they ran down the side of the mountain shouting out the joyous news that their god had not turned away from them.

The merchant watched them with detached amusement, but it is possible he would not have felt so superior, so apart from them, had he known that, in his own way, he too had shown his trust, or had realized, at that moment, that the performance of a miracle is the only way in which an unbeliever can affirm his faith.

84

the rattlesnake and
the scorpion

THE RATTLESNAKE AND the scorpion were usually to be found not far from each other, but the tie that bound them together was dislike rather than affection. When they met, as they managed to do a dozen times a day, the snake would draw back his head and flick out his tongue, while the scorpion reared up and got his stinger into position.

[166]

Then, one twilight as the snake was hunting among the rocks, he saw what he took to be a mouse crouching behind a stone. Instantly he coiled and sprang, but immediately he knew he had not swallowed a mouse as he had intended, but his enemy the scorpion instead. He tried to disgorge the scorpion, but he could not, and as he went to his den, he had a feeling of despair. "Anyway," he said to himself, "I've solved my hatred by swallowing my enemy. I won't dread meeting him any longer, because I'll know where he is at all times."

His hope was a false one, and as the days went by, his despair deepened until, at last, the thought that the hated scorpion was now a part of his own body was more than he could endure. He climbed the rocks as far as he could go and crawled on a ledge high in the air. "I'll destroy the scorpion even if I must destroy myself to do it," he said, and threw himself off the ledge onto the rocks below.

85

the squirrel and the trees

A FARMER WITH A GROVE
of walnut trees was enraged at a squirrel who was stealing
his nuts, and threatened to kill him if he didn't stop his
thefts. He said: "I wouldn't mind so much if you took
only enough for yourself, but you're too greedy for that.
You even steal nuts when you're not hungry and bury
them in the ground; and what's more, you never find
again a fraction of the nuts you hide away."

[168]

"It's true I steal more nuts than I need," said the squirrel; "but it isn't because I'm greedy; it's because squirrels are forgetful and foolish. But the nuts I bury and never find again aren't wasted, as you think; they sprout in the earth, and in time they come up and grow into trees as stately and fruitful as the parent that bore them."

He glanced anxiously at the farmer and then went on, "I don't know much about these matters, but it may be God made squirrels so impractical in order that His world would always be covered with beautiful, life-giving trees."

86

the fisherman and the hen

WHEN HE REACHED THE brook where he intended to fish, an angler found he had left his bait at home, but after considering matters, he thought he might be able to catch grasshoppers and use them instead. He got down on his hands and knees, but try as he would, he wasn't successful. He had about abandoned the idea of getting bait that way, when he saw an old hen in the grass, seeking her breakfast. As he watched, he realized the old hen, despite her infirmities, was a better grasshopper-catcher than he, for almost at once she pounced on a large, lively one and held it in her bill.

The fisherman crept toward the old hen, hoping to take the grasshopper from her before she could swallow it, but the hen, guessing his intention, flushed her wings and ran through the grass. She might have escaped if the fisherman had not thrown a stick at her. He caught her squarely, and she fell in the weeds, her tail feathers twitching from side to side.

He pulled the half-swallowed grasshopper from her throat, put it in his pocket, and turned away; but noticing how pathetic the old hen looked there in the grass, he picked her up and stroked her head. "Poor old thing!" he said. "I'm sorry for what I did just now!" He lifted her higher and rubbed his cheek against her wings. "I was a brute to hit you so hard," he said.

It was the first time the old hen had had any affection in years, and she lay back in the fisherman's arms making a clucking sound in her throat, until he put her down and went back to his fishing. Shortly thereafter, he dismissed the incident from his mind, being engaged with his own pleasures, so he was somewhat puzzled when he heard a soft, seductive noise behind him. He turned, and there was the old hen with another grasshopper in her beak. When she saw she had his attention, she moved away slowly, glancing back at him over her shoulder, awaiting his blow with resignation, since an old hen will put up with anything if you'll give her a little affection now and then.

87

the king
and the nature of man

AS HE GREW OLDER, THE
King of the Bretts was concerned more and more with
the nature of man, saying that before a ruler could
frame laws or govern justly, he should know what his
subjects were like; then at length one of the ministers
suggested a way of getting the knowledge he desired.

[173]

In his opinion, the true nature of man could be seen only when all hope was gone, when there was no longer any need for pretense. He suggested, therefore, that the king arrest fifty men at random and bring them to the great ballroom of the palace, where they would be locked up and told that within the hour they were to be beheaded. It was his suggestion, too, that the king hide behind a grating where he could observe what the prisoners did and hear what they said as they awaited their deaths.

This plan was put into action, and the king watched while the men were told that they had only an hour more of life. He noticed the prisoners were silent at first, too stunned to understand, and there seemed little difference between their individual natures; then, as they accepted their deaths as inevitable, they reacted in different ways: a dozen of the prisoners began to curse and shout. They picked up chairs and hurled them against the walls, breaking mirrors and vases, and tearing the tapestries down; but as fast as they destroyed the room, a dozen others walked behind them putting things to rights once more. In one corner a group knelt and prayed, while some of the others stood against one wall, indifferent to what awaited them, with a dignity more regal than anything the melancholy king had ever seen; and in the center of the room two prisoners fought fiercely for the honor of sitting in the king's chair during the few minutes of life that might remain to them.

[174]

The king turned to his minister and said, "How is it possible to make laws that will suit them all equally well? . . . Turn them loose, give them each a present, and tell them I never meant to harm them." Then his eyes went back to the noble, mean, ambitious, and cruel people who were his subjects.

A moment later he saw his soldiers open the door to the ballroom, but before the minister could give the order of release, one of the soldiers, mistaking his intention, said, "I beg you to spare the life of the young man standing beside the mantel. He comes from my village and we've been friends all our lives. He has a wife and children to look after."

The minister, knowing the king was still listening, continued the experiment. "If the king spares your friend," he said, "the number will be one short. Are you willing to take your friend's place?"

The soldier waited a long time, but at last he lowered his head and said yes. Then the king went to his apartment, where his musicians were waiting to play for him, but at their first note he rested his head in his hands and sat quietly, not knowing whether to laugh or cry.

88

the law of the foxes

THE FOXES AND THE
farmer ended their long war and signed a truce. The
farmer promised not to hunt down the foxes in the
future, and the foxes agreed not to steal from the farmer.
For a time things went smoothly, and then a hungry,
half-grown fox could no longer resist temptation, and he
stole a white hen from her roosting place on the premises
of the farmer. Being informed of this, the foxes brought
the thief to trial, inviting the farmer to attend in order
that he might see for himself that justice was done.

An old fox, acting as judge, pointed out how evil the crime had been, particularly since the roosting place of the hen had been known to all, and that any one of them, on any given occasion, could have taken her just as easily, but had not done so. At this the other foxes cried "Shame!" and demanded that the thief be given the severest punishment.

When the trial was over, the assembled foxes asked the farmer what he had thought of it, and the farmer said, "Tell me this: are you punishing the young fox because he stole my white hen or because you yourselves refrained from doing so?"

89

the farmhand and his judges

A FARMHAND WAS BROUGHT to trial for stealing a broken pump handle, a pickle bottle, and a box of colored crayons. The judge said, "Your thefts are senseless. You steal trivial things, things you don't even want."

"I know," said the prisoner. "I never benefit by what I take, and afterwards I'm ashamed and swear not to do it again; but there must be a reason for my behavior, and sometimes I feel I almost know what it is." He lifted his hands outward and said, "I wish my conduct were as easily understood as that of the squirrel."

The judge asked him to explain his last remark, and the farmhand went on: "Some months ago, a squirrel was gnawing my master's trees and doing them damage. He wasn't eating the bark, and he wasn't taking it away for his nest—he was just gnawing for no reason at all, or so I thought. His actions seemed as criminal to me as my actions seem to you, so I kept a lookout for him, and at last he stepped into the trap I'd made, just as I stepped into my master's trap.

"The little squirrel feared me because of what he had done, just as I fear you, and I could feel his heart pounding against my hands. I asked him why he had damaged the farmer's property, and he explained to me that the damage, from his viewpoint, wasn't senseless, as I thought. He said the teeth of a squirrel weren't like the teeth of a man. A man's teeth grow from top to bottom, and they stop growing when they reach their maturity; but a squirrel's teeth grow from the bottom upward, and continue to grow as long as he lives.

" 'But that doesn't explain why you gnaw trees,' I said.

" 'It does, master,' he answered. 'If I didn't gnaw trees, my teeth would grow so long that soon I wouldn't be able to close my mouth, and I'd die of starvation.' "

"What did you do then?" asked the judge.

"I told the squirrel I understood him, my nature being what it was," said the farmhand; "and I put him down and watched him run off into the woods." He looked at the judge and jury, but seeing their set, uncomprehending faces, he said, "I should be tried by a jury of squirrels, with whom I have something in common, and not by a jury of men who condemn me, not because of what I have done, but because of their own terrifying ignorance."

90

the strangers

THE WAGON PILED HIGH with household goods creaked and moved slowly down the village street. The man was driving while his wife and their children sat in the rear, half hidden by mattresses and cooking pots. The fact that the street was deserted did not mean the strangers were unobserved as they approached their new home, for hidden behind shutters, the people of the village watched resentfully. "What are those strangers doing here?" they asked one another. "Why did they pick our village to settle in?"

They were asking these questions even after the man and his family had moved into their new home. The strangers, knowing the uncertainty of their position, put themselves out to be agreeable, but the villagers ignored them. A little later, the villagers were no longer content with such a pensive attitude and began to speak their thoughts aloud. "We don't want you here," they said. "Why don't you go some place else?"

"Where?" asked the strangers. "Tell us, where?"

Still later, the villagers, seeing the defenselessness of the strangers, were no longer satisfied with words, and when the man and his family came out of their house, they were often met with a shower of old vegetables; but the stranger, whose whole life had been one of anxiety and sorrow, endured these things, telling his family that by and by the villagers would accept them, and they would be permitted to live there in peace, at last.

In this he was misguided, for one night when he went to the village, he was met by a crowd who threw rocks at him so violently that he had to turn back and run for his life. When he reached his own door, he called his wife and their children, and they came outside and stood with him against the wall. His forehead had been cut by a stone, and it was bleeding. When his wife saw the blood, she sat on the ground and began to cry, rocking from side to side. The stranger looked at the weeping woman, sighed, and spoke to the crowd outside his gate.

"Tell us," he began, "tell us how we have offended you."

The crowd shifted their feet and stared stupidly.

"What evil have we done you?" asked the man. "Why do you hate us? Why won't you let us live in peace?"

But nobody in the crowd spoke, for nobody could answer his questions.

91

the slave and the cart horse

A SLAVE WHO HAD BEEN beaten by his master came to the hut where his wife waited for him. He lay on a pallet, while the woman took a basin and filled it with water. He spoke after a time, answering the question his wife did not dare ask him: "It happened while I was working in the fields, near sunset. They had overloaded one of the cart horses, and the poor creature was hardly able to stand up. They were beating him with a whip, and although he was pulling with all his strength, he wasn't able to move the load out of the ruts in the field."

[182]

"Speak softer," said his wife. "The master might pass and hear you."

The slave lowered his voice and continued: "So I went to the master and told him that the horse couldn't carry such a load, and I asked him to take some of it off."

"Speak softer," said the woman. She bent over the slave and bathed his back with wet rags. "Speak softer. They'll whip you again if they hear what you're saying."

The slave got up and went to the door, to see that there was nobody outside; then he came and lay once more on the pallet. "I can't stand to see a horse cruelly treated. Horses always seem so helpless and pitiful to me."

When the woman spoke, her voice was so soft that it hardly carried to her husband's ears. "You did right," she said. "Horses aren't like us. They can't express themselves or stand up for their rights, and they have no way of defending themselves, like we have."

Then they looked into each others' eyes and sighed, thinking how fortunate they were and how cruelly horses were used, for no man can see his own misery clearly, and that is God's great mercy to us all.

92

the fox and the fur piece

TWO FOXES WERE RESTING in their cage at the zoo and talking about their brother who had escaped not long before, when they saw a young woman walking toward them. At once they sat up excitedly, for they saw that their lost brother was now draped around the shoulders of the lady.

"How lucky our brother is, compared with ourselves!" said one of the foxes. "See, what he has—traveling from place to place and enjoying the world, while we live our lives under the restrictions the keeper lays down for us! See how proudly our brother holds his ears! How brightly his eyes gleam! How, in his happiness, he smiles continuously!"

But the second fox, as the young lady came closer, saw that the eyes of his brother weren't real eyes at all, but were only bright pieces of glass, and that his ears and mouth were held in place and sealed up with brightly colored cement. When he realized the implications of these things, the second fox said, "I prefer the life we now lead, despite its restrictions and its small injustices, to the life of freedom our brother knows, a life in which one is not able to see, hear, or even speak for himself."

93

the prophets
and the mountains

THE TORTOISE, WHO HAD
seen the defeated mountain goats return to their homes
after their wars to enlighten the world, was talking with
his friend the lizard. "Oh, yes," he said. "I've lived a
long time, and I've watched a good many prophets rise
and fall. It all runs in the same pattern: first comes the
redeemer, then comes his mountain, and then comes
disaster."

The lizard did not understand and asked for a more complete explanation. "It's like this," continued the tortoise. "A redeemer isn't dangerous until he finds his particular mountain, but once he does, he climbs it and starts to preach; then the trouble begins. There's a strange connection between prophets and mountains, and there always has been."

The lizard moved on the wall so that the sun shone on him more warmly. "How would you cure the situation?" he asked. "Kill the prophets?"

"No, that won't work," said the tortoise. He yawned, burrowed deeper into the hot dust, and went on: "The only thing I see to do, if the world is ever to have peace, is to break the circle by tearing down the mountains."

"That's foolish, and you know it," said the lizard, stretching himself.

The tortoise said, "Of course it is, but not nearly so foolish as some of the other solutions which have been taken seriously during the two hundred years of my life."

94

the pious mantis

OF ALL THE CREATURES of the forest, there was none so devout as the female mantis. She would sit all day, her forefeet pressed together, her neck lifted toward heaven, while she said her prayers. The other insects considered her piety all the more praiseworthy because of the tragic life she had led, for hardly had she found a mate to share her love and keep her company than he died oddly, not long afterwards; then, one day the beetle made a discovery, and when next the mantis was in the mood for love, the other insects hid themselves and watched.

[188]

They saw her pause in her prayers at the exact instant her new mate approached and embraced her; then lowering her eyes from her contemplation of heaven, she turned meekly and chewed off his head. When this was accomplished, the mantis settled herself comfortably on her leaf and lifted her neck in an attitude of prayer, for there is no creature more cruel in her heart than a pious woman.

95

the prayer that was
almost answered

BEFORE HIM WAS A
cemetery, and behind him were the hunters who wanted
his skin, so the little fox jumped the wall and hid himself in a grave that had caved in at one side. He sighed
with relief when he heard the hunters stop at the wall
and turn back, knowing he had escaped disaster again;
but before he felt safe to return to his den, he was con-
fronted by a new danger, for a group of citizens, with
floral pieces in their arms, were approaching the grave
where he had found refuge.

When they reached it, they bared their heads, while

their leader began the address he had prepared. He said: "It is fitting that we observe this, the tenth anniversary of the death of Mrs. Ada Upshaw, the sainted founder of our association, with floral tributes testifying to our faith and devotion."

The congregation, at this point, sighed and touched their eyes with their handkerchiefs. "Oh, how we miss you, Mrs. Upshaw!" they said. "Oh, if you could only know how we grieve for you and long to have you with us again."

The orator bowed his head, and then went on with his address: "As the years go by, it becomes more and more evident what a loss our association has suffered in the departure from life of this great and estimable woman. Where can we find another as firm, as intolerant of sin, as generous with her time and money? Where can we find another as determined in crusading for the right, as aggressive, and yet as public-spirited?"

The orator stopped and looked about him, as if he challenged the others to take issue with him. He cleared his throat, but before he could continue his speech, the congregation began to weep. "Come back to us, Mrs. Upshaw!" they begged. "Come back to us, and guide us again!"

At that instant the fox saw a way to escape from his second dilemma of the afternoon, and he picked up a couple of bones and rattled them, groaning gently at the same time. There was a sudden silence, and the mourners stepped back from the grave, glancing nervously at one another. The leader quieted them. "Why are you frightened?" he asked. "It was nothing except the wind whistling through the gravestones." The congregation listened a moment, and then, reassured by the silence, they knelt at the graveside.

"Come back to us, dear Mrs. Upshaw!" they pleaded. "Don't leave us here to grieve! Oh, if it were only possible for you to come back from the grave, how happy we would be!"

At this moment, the fox heaved upward, and the slab above Mrs. Upshaw trembled and slid forward. Then he spoke in a shrill, petulant voice: "All right! I heard you! . . . I'll be with you just as soon as I can get my bones out of this shroud!"

But the people who had prayed so earnestly for her return did not wait to see Mrs. Upshaw after all. Instead, they screamed, threw away their flowers, and ran for the gate, trampling one another in their haste and tumbling over the wall. The fox emerged quickly from his hiding place, but he never got a fair look at the people he had frightened so badly, for at that moment they were disappearing over a small hill against the horizon, their screams muffled a little by the distance.

The fox laughed and trotted away in the direction of his lair. "It's a good thing that prayers aren't always answered," he said. "If they were, this would be even a more terrifying world to live in than it is now."

96

the unspeakable words

THERE WERE WORDS IN the Brett language considered so corrupting in their effect on others that if anyone wrote them or was heard to speak them aloud, he was fined and thrown into prison. The King of the Bretts was of the opinion that the words were of no importance one way or the other, and besides, everybody in the country knew them anyway; but his advisers disagreed, and at last, to determine who was right, a committee was appointed to examine the people separately.

At length everyone in the kingdom had been examined, and found to know the words quite well, without the slightest damage to themselves. There was then left only one little girl, a five-year-old who lived in the mountains with her deaf and dumb parents. The committee hoped that this little girl, at least, had never heard the corrupting words, and on the morning they visited her, they said solemnly: "Do you know the meaning of *poost, gist, duss,* and *feng?*"

The little girl admitted that she did not, and then, smiling happily, she said, "Oh, you must mean *feek, kusk, dalu,* and *liben!*"

Those who don't know the words must make them up for themselves.

97

aesop's last fable

AESOP, THE MESSENGER
of King Croesus, finished his business with the Delphians
and went back to the tavern where he had taken lodgings.
Later, he came into the taproom where a group of Delphians were drinking. When they realized who he was,
they crowded about him. "Tell us," they began, "is
Croesus as rich as people say?"

Aesop, since the habit of speaking in fables was so
strongly fixed in him, said, "I can best answer your question with a parable, and it is this: The animals gathered

together to crown their richest member king. Each animal in turn stated what he possessed, and it was soon apparent that the lion had the largest hunting preserves, the bee the most honey, the squirrel the largest supply of acorns, and so on; but when the voting began, the difficulty of arriving at a decision was plain to all, for to the bee, the nuts that represented the wealth of the squirrel were of no consequence; to the lion, the hay that the zebra and the buffalo owned was worthless; and the panther and the tiger set no value at all on the river that the crane and crocodile prized so highly."

Then Aesop called for his drink, looking into the faces of the Delphians with good-natured amusement. He said, "The moral of the fable is this: Wealth is an intangible thing, and its meaning is not the same to all alike."

The stolid Delphians looked at one another, and when the silence was becoming noticeable, one of them tried again: "How was the weather in Lydia when you left home?"

"I can best answer that question with another fable," said Aesop, "and it is this: During a rain storm, when the ditches were flooded and the ponds had overflowed their banks, a cat and a duck met on the road, and, wanting to make conversation, they spoke at the same instant. 'What a beautiful day this is,' said the delighted duck. 'What terrible weather we're having,' said the disgusted cat."

Again the Delphians looked at one another, and again there was silence. "The moral of that tale," said Aesop, "is this: What pleases a duck, distresses a cat." He poured wine into his glass and leaned against the wall, well satisfied with the start he had made in instructing the barbarous Delphians.

The Delphians moved uneasily in their seats, and after a long time, one of them said, "How long are you going to be here?"

"That," said Aesop, "can best be answered in the Fable of the Tortoise, the Pelican, and the Wolf. You see, the pelican went to visit his friend the tortoise and promised to remain as long as the latter was building his new house. Then one day as they were working together, with the tortoise burrowing and the pelican carrying away the dirt in his pouch, the wolf came on them unexpectedly, and—"

But Aesop got no farther, for the Delphians had surrounded him and were, an instant later, carrying him toward the edge of the cliff on which the tavern was built. When they reached it, they swung him outward and turned him loose, and Aesop was hurled to the rocks below, where he died. "The moral of what we have done," they explained later, "is so obvious that it needs no elaboration."

98

iadmon and aesop

AFTER THEY HAD KILLED
the slave Aesop, the Delphians were uneasy in their
minds and consulted the Oracle of Apollo. The oracle
said that in order to cleanse themselves of guilt, they
must pay damages to the owner of Aesop. Accordingly,
the Delphians announced their willingness to do this,
and Iadmon, the grandson of the former Iadmon who
had owned Aesop, came forward to claim his damages.

[198]

He was a young man who had long since spent his inheritance, and this windfall of unexpected money was a pleasant occurrence indeed, but to his surprise, he found that Aesop, after his death, had taken on a certain importance. People went about mourning for him, repeating his sayings, and predicting that his like wouldn't be seen again in Lydia for many a day. "How could the Delphians have done such a thing?" they asked. "How could they murder harmless old Aesop?"

Young Iadmon listened to these things and thought in bewilderment, "Why do they make such a fuss over Aesop? I can't see that his life was of any particular importance. I think the Delphians acted wisely in throwing him off the cliff." He jingled the gold coins in his pocket. They made a comforting and a convincing sound. "What else could the Delphians have done?" he said. "How could they have acted otherwise?"

99

the unique quality of truth

WHEN THE OLD SCHOLAR heard that Truth was in the country, he decided to find her, as he had devoted his life to studying her in all her forms. He set out immediately, and at last he came upon the cottage in the mountains where Truth lived alone. He knocked on the door, and Truth asked what he wanted. The scholar explained who he was, adding that he had always wanted to know her and had wondered a thousand times what she really was like.

Truth came to the door soon afterwards, and the scholar saw that the pictures he had formed of her in his imagination were wrong. He had thought of Truth as a gigantic woman with flowing hair who sat nobly on a white horse, or, at the very least, as a sculptured heroic figure with a wide white brow and untroubled eyes. In reality, Truth was nothing at all like that; instead, she was merely a small, shapeless old woman who seemed made of some quivering substance that resembled india rubber.

"All right," said the old lady in a resigned voice. "What do you want to know?"

"I want to know what you are."

The old lady thought, shook her head, and answered, "That I don't know. I couldn't tell you to save my life."

"Then have you any special quality that makes you an individual?" asked the scholar. "Surely you must have some characteristic that is uniquely yours."

"As a matter of fact, I have," said the old lady; then, seeing the question on the scholar's lips, she added, "I'll show you what I mean. It's easier than trying to explain."

The shapeless old woman began to bounce like a rubber ball, up and down on her doorstep, getting a little higher each time she struck the floor. When she was high enough for her purpose, she seized the woodwork above her door and held on; then she said, "Take hold of my legs and walk back the way you came, and when you know what my unique quality is, shout and let me know."

The old scholar did as he was told, racking his brains in an effort to determine what quality it was that distinguished Truth. When he reached the road, he turned

around, and there in the distance was Truth still clinging
to the woodwork above her door.

"Don't you see by this time?" she shouted. "Don't you
understand now what my particular quality is?"

"Yes," said the old scholar. "Yes, I do."

"Then turn my legs loose and go on home," said
Truth in a small petulant voice.